THE BLACK BOX

OTHER TITLES BY JAMES CHAMBERS

The Engines of Sacrifice
Resurrection House
On the Night Border
On the Hierophant Road

OTHER eSPEC BOOKS TITLES BY JAMES CHAMBERS

THE CORPSE FAUNA SERIES
The Dead Bear Witness
Tears of Blood
The Dead in Their Masses
The Eyes of the Dead

SYSTEMA PARADOXA SERIES
Devil in the Green (Volume 6)

OTHER eSPEC BOOKS TITLES INCLUDING JAMES CHAMBERS

After Punk
The Side of Good/The Side of Evil
Gaslight & Grimm
Best of Bad-Ass Faeries
Awakened Modern
Society for the Preservation
of CJ Henderson

DEFENDING THE FUTURE SERIES
Dogs of War
Man and Machine
In Harm's Way
Best of Defending the Future

BEYOND THE CRADLE SERIES
If We Had Known
Footprints in the Stars

JAMES CHAMBERS

VOX ASTRA

THE BLACK BOX

PUBLISHED BY
eSpec Books LLC
Danielle McPhail,
Publisher
PO Box 242,
Pennsville, New Jersey 08070
www.especbooks.com

ISBN: 978-1-949691-97-9
ISBN (ebook): 978-1-949691-96-2

Copy Editor: Greg Schauer, John L. French
Cover Design: Mike McPhail, McP Digital Graphics
Interior Design: Danielle McPhail,
Sidhe na Daire Multimedia
www.sidhenadaire.com

Cover Art: The final eclipse © GrandeDuc,
www.shutterstock.com

Interior Icon: Star Symbol Set2 © tichaporn,
www.fotolia.com

FOR MY DAD,
WHO INTRODUCED ME TO SCIENCE FICTION

Acknowledgments

I am grateful to the editors and publishers who gave me the opportunities to write these stories and first published them, especially to Danielle Ackley-McPhail, Mike McPhail, Peter Worthy, and Bruce Gehweiller, who created the world of Byanntia. Much gratitude goes to the readers who supported the various anthologies in which they appeared and those who continue to support my writing and read my books. Endless thanks go to my family for their unflagging encouragement and patience in selflessly allowing me the time and space an author needs to write and for listening to me ramble about story ideas and publishing drama.

Contents

Introduction
Never Less Than Stellar

I have been on this journey a long time, as an author, an editor, and a publisher. Along the years I have worked with many authors, but few have remained with me along this path as long as James Chambers.

There is a reason for that.

In 2005 I produced my first anthology, *No Longer Dreams*, published by Lite Circle Books. On the recommendation of the late and long-missed CJ Henderson, I included a story by an author who was new to me. That story was "Law of the Kuzzi" and the author, of course, was James Chambers.

I have never regretted that decision. In fact, of the twenty-two anthologies I have edited and/or published directly, I have invited James to contribute to eighteen of them. He has never disappointed. Regardless of the genre or theme, his writing has delivered a unique and talented voice to every project. Often, he has even garnered the coveted first or last slot in the collection, where wise editors place their two best stories.

I must say, I have yet to find the challenge that James Chambers has failed to meet, something that cannot even be said by the iconic CJ Henderson, from whom I have rejected at least one story in my career. Unheard of, I assure you.

I am honored to have curated and/or published many of the stories in this collection. Well... to be truthful—as of the publication of this volume—all of the stories in this collection. I doubt there is anything James could write that I would not at least be willing to consider.

With complete honesty, I can say that I have never worked with a more talented and versatile author. And believe me, I have worked with some of the best.

As you read this collection, I hope you find the same level of enjoyment that I always have.

Regards,

Danielle Ackley-McPhail

War Movies

We watched movies underground while the surface burned.

Down in our rabbit holes, the sound of the bombs never reached us, but the earth shook with their impact while we sat in the dark and watched moving pictures flicker across a silver screen. We knew what kind of hell rained down over our heads: one full of heat, shrapnel, and death, worse than any atrocity long-dead, special-effects wizards had left for us on film. When enough skybusters exploded at once, they set the air on fire. We wondered what we'd find left of our home and of the Frek when we deployed up-earth, whenever our time came. Some of the guys worried that our twelve brutal weeks in boot camp and three more in psychprep would go to waste without any of us ever seeing so much as a skirmish. Other guys hoped for that. I knew better. We were weapons, and the Army didn't make weapons it didn't intend to use.

When the movies started, I knew we'd see action before long. All they showed us were war movies and monster movies—the blockbusters, the classics, the cult favorites, and even a few hits from the summer before the Frek dropped down and started us fighting for our lives.

The most gruesome movies ran two or three times a week. During the day, we bled out our frustrations in the gyms and training rooms, and at night we stoked them again with images of violence and alienness, of combat and heroism, of strangeness, mystery, and bloody struggle for survival. The picture shows were part of a slow burn lit to keep our rage simmering. They reinforced the narrative we'd learned in boot camp. They showed us again and again that only country and fellowship mattered and that aliens like the Frek were nothing more than slavering, man-eating, evil beasts hell-bent on raping our planet and enslaving us. We heard the message loud and clear.

One night a PFC from Kansas joked about why, if they were so hot for the "sky-fi stuff," they never showed E.T. Without missing a beat, the guy next to him described in detail how he would shove a grenade down E.T.'s throat and "blow his fucking heartlight the fuck home and fuck needing to use the phone." Everyone laughed so hard they stopped the movie.

The strangest part of it is when you see some of these guys from on-screen walking around in officer's dress. Seeing them on television, like when General Eastwood and General McQueen address the nation, gives you a touch of that uncanny-valley sensation, but in person, they make your skin crawl. Colonel Connery, CO for our rabbit hole, looks exactly like the real deal, circa 1968, except you know nothing from back then still knocks around his head, only ideas of death and killing and keeping our morale high. They clone them so well, I bet even their wives and girlfriends, if they were still alive, wouldn't know the difference. It gets the guys' attention, sure enough. No one's mind ever wanders when the colonel speaks in his powerful, Scottish accent, and whenever they run one of his old movies, a handful of guys always hit him up for autographs, asking how he liked shooting the love scenes.

He smirks and nods as if he knows.

It's a hell of psyche-out.

No bombing for two days.

Our orders came through: surface clean-up for most of the men, but not for my platoon. We pulled special duty. We were to rendezvous with a Special Forces unit that had collected what our orders described as a "valuable artifact," secure it from them, and bring it to Camp Scott, on the double-quick, of course.

Leaving our rabbit hole, however, involved a process.

First, advance teams surfaced and reported back on up-earth conditions. Then everyone got booster shots against possible contagion from Frek remains, took anti-rad pills, and equipped themselves with live ammo and full-integrity body armor to replace what we'd damaged in training. Centcom had shipped us in and tucked us away only days ahead of the campaign to sterilize the Eastern seaboard then left us down-earth for two months, like cicadas waiting to hatch from the ground when the weather turned hot, and we were eager to go. Even the guys who'd been dreading the day they'd see action looked relieved to finally do something.

Colonel Connery made the rounds while we suited up.

Captain Willis and Captain Weathers followed him.

They helped with our gear. They steadied our nerves and tried to keep us from thinking too much about the blasted wasteland that waited on the surface.

I snapped the last of my armor in place, checked my ammunition, and waited for my platoon to finish suiting up. I was their sergeant. I tried not to think about what that meant. I'd had weeks to ruminate on it. Now was time to act.

Colonel Connery reviewed our orders with me and said he was grateful to have a man like me in his division. I wondered how much of that came from what they'd programmed into his brain on the clone farm or if he'd thought up any of it on his own. I guess it didn't matter one way or the other. His pep talk was protocol. When he finished, he slapped me on the back, said he'd keep a good cigar waiting for me, then walked off into the crowd of soldiers.

By then, my platoon had gathered at the elevator. The long ride to the surface passed in silence. Anticipation poured off my men in waves. They were good soldiers: Abernathy, Barnes, Champ, Foster, Itgen, Marvin, Morris, Smith, and Testa.

And me, Colin Rook.

They were my soldiers: Rook's Raiders.

I hoped we'd all come back together.

I knew we wouldn't.

Riding up-earth, it seemed we'd always been fighting the Frek, as if the pre-invasion world had only ever existed in movies and dreams, and no time before my first day in boot camp had been real. I couldn't remember the day I decided to enlist or even when the Frek invasion began. Like everyone else, though, I knew their first assault had come without warning. We hadn't even known that the Frek, or any other alien life, existed until they attacked us.

Even now, no one really understands why they invaded Earth.

I lean toward the mistake theory: the Frek thought there were no intelligent species here, and by the time they figured out otherwise, they'd gone too far to change course. If all Frek invasions are alike, they're pretty much impossible to stop once they're underway. Frek females the size of attack helicopters give birth to about 500 young at a time. Frek children pop out of the womb in little, curled up bundles no bigger than cantaloupes, but they grow to the size of lambs in about three days, and they're more vicious than badgers. The first anyone knew we were under attack, pregnant Frek mothers, already in labor, dropped from the sky and popped out killing machines. They dropped about thirty mothers per continent, and within days 15,000 hungry, newborn Frek bastards shocked the world. What's worse, about thirty Frek out of every litter are female. Those things mature, mate, and reproduce in a matter of weeks. Soon as we caught on to that, we made hunting the brood-mothers a priority. That's when the scorched-earth campaigns began.

We started with nukes. The blasts burned the Freks to cinders, but the radiation barely slowed the survivors. It did have the benefit of sterilizing them, which made them easier to fight without worrying about picking up some Frek microbe that would blind you or turn your organs to slush. So far, the white-coat grunts have identified about thirteen separate bacterial strains the Frek brought to Earth, seven of which kill humans. They're working on cures and vaccines, but anything better than the crude, imperfect immunization shots they give us in boot camp is a long way off. You catch a Frek death germ, you may as well throw yourself in front of a firegun for all the medics can help you. Thank God the Frek bugs haven't mutated to airborne or human-to-human transmission yet.

Centcom switched to skybusters, which had about the same effect as nukes but without spreading so much fallout. The sterilization campaigns picked up in earnest then. Africa is clear of

Freks now. The thing is, it's also pretty much clear of humans. No one's really sure if we won that battle. The Frek control half of Asia and all of South America. Bombing runs 24/7 keep them in check. Australia has fared pretty well, with about half the country still habitable and mostly Frek free. Europe and North America still hang in the balance. That's where Rook's Raiders and a million other grunts come in. We were trained in the western deserts where the Frek never came and then shipped east and north where the Frek are the densest. Now it was time to go see what we could kill.

Fighting Frek isn't easy. The children have skin like a beetle's carapace, and they can launch razor-sharp quills from their upper legs. Shooting the bastards five or six times usually drops them. Grenades work better. The only thing that makes it manageable is they're stupid and impulsive. They tend to come running straight at you. They're fast, though. Let one through, there's not much you can do but pray somebody's got your back.

The brood-mothers are worse. Soon as they finish giving birth, they're back on all ten feet fighting. They spit streams of the vilest soup imaginable. It'll burn you bad. Allergic soldiers go anaphylactic and drop dead in seconds. The worst of the germs comes from the birther spit. You might survive being doused, but you'll spend a couple of months in D and Q, shaved hairless and having layers of skin flash-burned off you, while robot medics prick you and pop tubes into all your available orifices three times a day.

The mothers are uglier than the kids too. They lumber around like octopi with stilts rammed into their tentacles. Their flat heads stretch into squares, and their five big, red eyes never blink. I've never seen one in person, but they showed us plenty of vid records in boot camp. Every grunt and officer receives a camera chip implanted in their skull beside their left eye, making every soldier a cameraman. That's created a bounty of raw battlefield footage, and the top brass uses it liberally.

That shit'll give you nightmares.

✳

We made our rendezvous, and my first thought was someone at Centcom has a wicked sense of humor. That's the only explanation I can muster for why they cloned Peter Lorre to lead the Special Forces team. Not only him, either. The other spooks hung back in the shadows, but I swore I saw Karloff and Price in captain's bars, Rathbone, a major. We met them inside a dark, gloomy, blasted-out warehouse, and I had to choke back a laugh. The movies those guys made were the ones I liked best: the classic monster flicks. They were the only ones with a touch of style to them. They were gruesome, violent, and morbid, but they had real stories, romances, and none of that formulaic, jingoistic cheerleading in almost every war movie we saw. Those old fright flicks came closer to reminding me of why I fought than anything else we watched. That's because the heroes in those movies—and yeah, sometimes the monster was the hero, like in *Frankenstein* or *The Creature from the Black Lagoon*—the heroes were almost always noble.

I could buy that in a monster movie.

Not so much in the combat pics. In those, the hero died in the end way too often. Anyway, I'd seen fifty guys wash out of boot camp for everything from cowardice to dementia to battlefield incontinence, and I knew soldiers weren't always noble. So, it struck me funny about Peter Lorre being cloned for Special Forces. He never played the hero in the horror shows. The thing about him, he unnerved you even if you didn't recognize him. A tic shook his head every few seconds, and his eyes looked rheumy enough to slide from their sockets. Considering the Special Forces guys fought in the dark and had little contact with anyone but the enemy, the creepier, the better, I guess. Not that the Frek cared, but I guess it mattered to someone.

With Lorre, they even got the voice right.

"Sergeant," he said. "We have your valuable cargo, ready for transport to Camp Scott. Are you prepared to take possession?"

"Ready, willing, and able," I told him.

"Excellent. Your papers?"

I handed him our orders. He skimmed them as he led me to the back of the huge transport truck, then he opened one of the rear doors. Inside sat a canister about twelve feet in diameter and roughly twenty feet long, spattered with mud and other dried gunk. It looked like a rusty, oversized oil drum. Sealed up tight and strapped down solid enough to stay put even if the truck rolled, it filled almost the entire cargo space. I'd never seen anything like it.

"What the hell you got in there?" I asked.

"We have captured one of the enemy's brood-mothers before labor and have trapped it in stasis in this tank. Frek bodies are quite pliable once they're subdued."

I guess I made a face or didn't speak for too long because Captain Lorre's expression grew even more anxious. He pulled out a white handkerchief and wiped sweat from his brow. "Are you deaf, Sergeant? I tell you we have captured one of the enemy birthers and have trapped it in this tank, yet you have nothing to say."

I'd heard him fine. No one had ever taken one of the Frek birthers alive. I thought we'd have heard the news.

"It is top secret, of course, which is why we must get the prisoner inside Camp Scott as quickly as possible. You and your men only have to drive this truck home, like good chauffeurs. Do not interfere with the canister. For God's sake, don't try to open it, or there will be horrible consequences. Absolutely horrible."

"You coming with us?"

He shook his head and wiped his brow again, and I saw why his unit had to pass the baton. Captain Lorre's sleeve pulled back from the hem of his glove, uncovering about eight blood blisters on his wrist, a sign of Frek infection. The rest of his unit must have been contaminated too. They'd probably caught the germ while subduing the birther. Word was when Special Forces picked up a Frek bug, they didn't bother coming in for triage. They simply ran suicide missions to kill as many Frek as possible before they expired. I felt a little sad for the captain, but in the end, he was only a clone. No doubt there were other Special Forces "monster units" running around out there. Centcom hated to waste a good clone matrix once they'd developed it. Captain Lorre handed me the keys to the truck and turned to rejoin his unit. I called him back before he disappeared into the shadows.

"Hey," I said. "They forget Lugosi?"

The captain smiled. "Oh, no, they could never forget Lugosi, but I'm sad to have to tell you he didn't make it. He's in the canister with the prisoner."

Morris drove. I rode shotgun.

In the back with the trophy were Abernathy, Champ, Marvin, and Testa. Barnes, Foster, and Smith rode the gun positions mounted behind the cab. Itgen sat between Morris and me and worked up a sweat navigating.

We had maps and GPS and high-level training in dead reckoning. Only problem was all that was keyed to geography that no longer existed. A few days of skybusters had chewed up the landscape and spit it back out in a bold, new arrangement. Even when we followed the compass, we kept coming to roads turned into craters, bridges reduced to splinters, and buildings blasted across every inch of ground, creating a litter of obstacles where the map showed clear paths. Camp Scott should've been a six-hour drive from our rendezvous with Special Forces, but we'd covered only a quarter of the distance in that time. Every so often, we spied the dark specks of surveillance drones coasting past the horizon. At one point, we passed a rabbit hole and thought we might stop for help, but an off-target skybuster had cracked its lid and let the Frek in. We knew what we'd find down there. We moved on, fast.

Another hour and we covered maybe fifteen more miles. We'd started in daylight. Now dusk crept in along the horizon. I debated whether we should push on or stake a defensible position in the rubble. Neither option appealed to me. Being indoors at a secure location overnight was Survival 101. While I mulled that over, Foster popped off a dozen rounds into the shadows of a broken building, and everyone snapped alert with weapons ready.

Something moved behind a pile of debris. Several other somethings followed it.

About thirty Frek bastards skittered out from beneath the rocks and charged us. How the hell they survived the sky-busters, I'll never know, but I didn't worry too much about having an opportunity to rectify that. I climbed onto the hood of the truck and opened fire.

Barnes and Smith kicked in with the fireguns. The rest of the men started lobbing grenades from the rear of the vehicle. One of them went wild and ripped a grapefruit-sized hole in the truck's armor. Everything turned fiery and frantic and sounded far away once explosions numbed my eardrums. Most of the Frek were dying, but the ones that made it through, instead of coming for us, tried to claw their way through the side of the truck. They must have sensed the birther in there. The truck's armor slowed them enough to make them easy pickings, and we ended the skirmish soon enough. Not a casualty among us, but the Frek were all dead.

We regrouped and drove off.

I screamed at Morris to go faster and kept screaming until we were far from where we'd been attacked. His ears had to be as dead as mine by then, but he got the message. When the ride smoothed out, Itgen and I took up the map and tried to calculate our safest route.

The best we could do was hope we'd find the shortest.

Darkness fell, and Morris kept driving.

Barnes, Foster, and Smith popped on their night eyes.

The truck's headlights were bright, but the dense, pervasive darkness swallowed up the light. Around midnight we passed an unexploded skybuster sitting in a crater and drove around it. Rare, but it happened. A dud igniter, or maybe someone didn't arm it properly. Eventually, it would blow. They always did.

Half an hour later, we stopped.

Bad news.

Abernathy and Testa had found holes in the stasis tank. Something was leaking out. They refused to ride with it. I got out and climbed into the cargo space.

Shrapnel from where a stray grenade had blown a hole in our armor during the skirmish had perforated the skin of the tank. The sludge dripping out was the color of cornhusks, probably a combination of Frek blood and whatever had been pumped in there to keep the birther alive. There wasn't much, but if it was contaminated, it was plenty.

My men looked to me for answers.

I had no good ones.

I told them to look for a tire repair kit. When they found it, I dug out its largest self-adhesive patch and slapped it onto the canister. It held, but it barely covered the three holes, and I saw it would peel off as soon as it got too damp from the leakage.

There weren't enough footholds outside the cargo trailer for everyone to ride on the exterior. It would've been too dangerous in the dark. Hit a bad bump, you could lose someone and never notice. As ugly as it sounded, some of us would have to ride with the tank.

No one liked it, but they accepted it, especially when I told them I'd be riding there with them. I ordered Abernathy and Testa to squeeze in up front, then climbed into the trailer with Champ and Marvin.

Before we closed the doors, before Morris even started the engine, I heard something buzz by overhead. Its high-pitched whine identified it as a surveillance drone. Maybe they were searching for us because we were so late. Two small orange lights circled in the black sky. Between them blinked a single red light. The drone passed over us low before it rose and began circling. I was watching it when the entire truck lurched, and I almost fell out.

It felt like we'd hit a huge bump, but we weren't moving. The truck shook again. This time I saw why. It bounced with the tank. The metal container vibrated and shook, and every few seconds, it jolted in one direction or another like the birther inside wanted to pound its way out.

The makeshift patch popped off, and goop spurted the inside of the truck. Champ and Marvin almost knocked me over on their way out. I jumped down, and we all drew our weapons. The others came around from the front, armed and frightened. We watched the tank rock and rattle and wondered if it would hold.

They never should've made me a sergeant. I don't think like most soldiers. I never bought all the way into the official story of how things are. When someone tries too hard to sell me something, it makes me suspicious, and that's what all those movies were down our rabbit hole. A nonstop sales pitch to keep us on board with how the honchos wanted us to see things. The clones worked like a charm in that regard, tricking soldiers and civilians into believing reality was exactly like the movies and vice versa, leading us deeper into the story, distracting us from asking questions, so we would always fight the Frek with steady fervor.

Not that I doubted we were fighting for our lives; I knew we were.

Only I wasn't sure we'd been given all the information. When a movie's based on true events, there's tons of stuff they leave out to make the story more exciting. For example, behind every war, people pull the strings, and sometimes they do it for their own benefit and damn the world and everyone in it. The movies never showed those people.

When the tank settled down, everyone let out the breath they'd been holding.

I hopped into the trailer, ignoring my men's shouts for me to stay clear.

I walked up to the tank and banged on it.

Whatever was inside banged back.

That gave me a shudder. The guys got quiet.

I tapped the metal again, and again got a response.

Another two raps got me two right back.

I looked at my men. "No fucking way that's a Frek birther in there."

No one said a thing.

I saw in their faces that they all wanted to close the thing up, get back in the truck, and dump it at Camp Scott. Already done wouldn't be fast enough for them.

I wanted that too, but even more, I wanted to know what the hell was in the can.

Unclipping the flashlight from my belt, I walked around the damaged side. Standing on a field box, I stepped up eye level with the holes and flashed the light in. No more had dribbled out, and what was there was drying to a crust, but the unmistakable stench of Frek came pouring out. Through the punctured metal, I saw only darkness and a yellowish shine from my light reflecting off the goop.

A shadow moved inside.

My light flashed off a patch of iridescent Frek skin.

An eye filled up one of the holes and peeped out at me.

Screaming, I stumbled backward, lost my balance, and fell. Abernathy and Barnes bolted into the trailer, grabbed me, then dragged me out, spilling me onto the ground while the rest of the men leveled their weapons toward the canister.

I told them to stand down.

I told them we'd been lied to.

I told them what I'd seen through the hole in the metal.

A human eye.

Aside from me, Barnes, and Testa, no one thought opening the tank was a good idea. After I calmed down, I figured the monster unit's Lugosi was alive in there. It made sense, but it didn't sit right with me. Still, I thought we should try to rescue him. The rest of the men wanted to push on to Camp Scott, and since those were our orders, we did so.

A few miles farther along, we reached impassable ground.

Must have been a hundred skybusters dropped there during the bombing because not an unbroken spot of earth remained as far as we could see in any direction, except back the way we came. We couldn't raise anyone on the radio, probably due to residual radiation in the air over the blasted zone. Itgen and I scrutinized the map but found no sure way around. A river blocked our way to the south, rough hills to the north, and east was back the way we came.

While we sat on our options, the Frek came again.

Whatever survived the last bombing campaign must have tracked us most of the night. They came from behind, out of the dark. Only Abernathy keeping watch with his night eyes stopped them from overrunning us before we knew they were there.

We opened fire and scrambled for the truck.

Morris revved the engine.

Most of us made it on board. Frek bastards got Champ and Marvin and dragged them out of sight.

A rain of quills clattered against the armor. Morris floored the gas, turned us around, and drove us head-on toward the line of running Freks. They crunched under the tires and splatted against the armored sides, but a lot managed to hang on. We were covered with them, and they did their best to tear the truck open. They wanted to kill us, I'm sure, but more so, they wanted whatever the tank contained. Whether or not we ever reached Camp Scott, I couldn't let that happen. I leaned over to Morris and told him where to go and then prayed we could hold off the Frek long enough to get there.

By the time we reached the unexploded skybuster, we'd lost Barnes, Smith, and Testa to the Frek. Morris slammed to a stop so close to the bomb, we almost bumped it. The effect was immediate: the Frek fled, scrambled back, and circled around us. They knew enough to fear the skybuster. The break from fighting brought temporary relief, but then it sunk in that I'd only achieved a standoff.

In the fleeting quiet, drones buzzed overhead. There were four of them now, orange lights hovering like eyes, red lights blinking like stars. I no longer thought they'd been sent to find and help us. They were there to watch and record. We were on; it was our big moment.

I tried the radio again. Only static, maybe due to interference from the drones.

Without help, I saw only one way out.

If we gave the Frek what they wanted, they'd slaughter us the moment they had it. I looked at Foster, Itgen, and Morris and saw they'd each concluded the same thing. We had enough ammo to hold off the enemy for a couple of hours, no more. The Frek would get us and the tank before dawn.

We couldn't allow it.

Rook's Raiders wound up in a war movie instead of a monster movie. We'd get to die for our mission instead of killing the monster and living to see the next dawn.

The four of us climbed into the back of the truck and untied the tank. It shook and jolted as we worked, knocking us off-balance. Whatever was inside, it wanted out. Maybe it sensed what we had in mind. Foster dropped out and examined the skybuster, locating the access panel that would allow manual detonation. He gave us the thumbs-up. With the cargo doors open, the Frek knew what we planned, and they didn't like it. They came at us in a biting wave. We fought, but they out-numbered us. Seven Frek bastards got Foster as he pulled a grenade. He dropped it live. It exploded beneath the truck, knocking me, Morris, and Itgen to the ground and driving the Frek back. But the blast hit the exposed tank too.

The seal at the end cracked.

Fluid squirted out.

The Frek closed on us again.

The thing inside the tank pounded against the lid, shoving it upward by inches.

In the sky, eight drones circled now, each one watching from a different place, a different angle, recording us, even as we recorded everything we saw through our implanted cameras. I wondered who was watching and why they didn't send help.

Then the lid popped off the tank and slammed against the skybuster.

From the opening, two limbs emerged: one Frek, the other human. The massive thing inside squeezed itself from the canister, pushing a wash of viscous goop with it as it came. When it unfolded, stood on its ten legs, and raised the flat disk of its body into the air, the sight sent us reeling. It throbbed and pulsated as if gasping for breath. Dangling from its underbelly were eight bodies at the end of pulpy tubes. Two were miniature Frek birthers. The other six were human. Lugosi hung there, staring down at us, and so many others: McQueen, Willis, Weathers, even Colonel Connery. Each unfinished figure awaited the breath of life and its brain to start working at full capacity. They looked frightened and half alert.

The worst part of it hit me the moment Itgen and Morris turned their guns on me.

One of those dangling, dripping horrors possessed my face.

I ran toward the skybuster even as my men opened fire.

I felt the punch of the slugs and started to go numb, but my fingers were already clutching the wires. I pressed them together and clicked the switch.

The skybuster turned the world to fire.

Down the rabbit holes, soldiers watch movies while the surface burns.

I take no interest in them now that I wear captain's bars. On the nights they show my movies, I stay in my quarters and read technical manuals. Centcom told me that with time the memories should fade. They haven't, though. There's something about me, a flaw in my matrix that keeps me from forgetting.

They never should've made me a captain.

General Eastwood was there to hand me my bars and congratulate me when I came back online at the clone farm.

"You've done good, son, and we got it all on film," he said. "The folks at home loved it around the world. You're international now."

They told me intelligence suspected the existence of the Frek in the canister but had never seen one up close. It grew clones of captured soldiers. Once the Frek realized how clones helped sustain our war efforts, they decided to use them against us. They had captured several clone farms in South America, which gave them all the data they needed. They couldn't master our technology, but they found an organic way to create clones. Then they set out to infiltrate our troops by sending decoys into the field. They'd started with Special Forces. Captain Lorre and the rest of his monster unit had been bogus, infected with Frek germs to self-destruct. They had given us a Trojan horse and trusted us to ferry it inside Camp Scott. I'd been among the decoys only because the Frek had captured the clone farm where I'd been brought online. Our real cargo had been the recovered torch from the Statue of Liberty, a "valuable artifact" like our orders had said. Now it was gone, and we had a whole new front on which to fight the Frek. I guess they hadn't counted on their stray bastards fouling up their plot by trying to rescue what their senses told them was a brood-mother.

Me and all my "others" got bucked up to captain for my "quick thinking and decisive action in the field." I hadn't known until then that I was a clone.

"It's better that way," General Eastwood had said. "You had some popular movies before the Frek landed, but we had to test run your matrix. Make sure you were functional, see what kind of ratings you got. You start out a sergeant for a couple of runs, and we see if you break out into a more popular role. We're at war, sure, but that doesn't mean we can't entertain people to keep their spirits high. You passed with flying colors. Now we'll start reaping the cumulative benefits of your experience. That's how we'll beat the Frek. Sooner or later, we'll find the way to a decisive victory. But it's a hell of an adventure getting there, and we've got to keep the populace on board with the war. If it sinks in how dire things really are, it would be too demoralizing. People might want to surrender. We won't let that happen."

I asked him when I would see my men again, if they would keep my unit together. A puzzled look came over General Eastwood's face, and he smiled like a patient father as he told me, "They were extras, kid. Extras don't come back. Extras get recast."

He saluted me and walked away.

Before he stepped through the door, I asked, "General, are we winning?"

Without looking back, he said, "Of course, we're winning. We're the heroes, son."

He seemed so certain.

I remember a lot of things I'm not supposed to, but I don't remember how long we've really been fighting the Frek. I think of how easily it came to me to sacrifice myself and my men by blowing the skybuster. It reminds me that sometimes Frankenstein's monster was the hero too. Now the whole world feels like a haunted house: not everything here is what it seems, and ghosts are everywhere.

That's why I don't watch the movies anymore.

I can't sit down there in the dark while the ground rumbles and shakes above us, sit there with the good men who are winning the war against the Frek, but who won't come back when they die, won't ever see victory, won't ever be known for their sacrifice. I can't sit there in the dark with the extras. They're heroes too, but they're trapped in a war movie, and I'm trapped in a horror show.

A Beach on Nellus

Sarah Nuhr FitzRose spotted the missing planet cruiser, *Mercury*, submerged beneath clear water at the end of a trail gouged through the jungle to the narrow beach and into the bright, rippling surf. A tongue flick to the sheath of her helmet lit her augmented reality display. Among the illuminated strings of data blinked a red icon, confirming the proximity of the beacon sewn into the abducted girl's clothes.

Sarah scouted the shore for a place to land. The next nearest scrap of earth on Nellus lay 660 miles away across a world 98 percent covered by ocean. She banked the glider and eyed a sandy strip fringed by vine-draped trees and elephantine leaves. Cutting altitude until spray kicked up, she fired her braking thrusters then skimmed her glider's belly across the surface to slow her approach. The glider lurched sideways. Sarah wrestled it on course, skipping from wave crest to wave crest. She nosed down, plunging the glider beneath the fluid's skin. The sharp drop in speed pitched her forward, knocking her helmet against the cockpit glass. Caught by the undertow, her glider jerked sideways into shallow waters, then spun and skidded up the beach, furrowing sand until it stopped hard against a thick wall of entwined tree trunks.

The glider's systems malfunctioned and winked out.

The echo of the crash rang in Sarah's ears.

When the shock faded, she punched the cockpit release, lifted the glass, and spilled out onto the soft sand. Wrestling her feet under her, she stood, surveyed her landing, and found the glider's frame crumpled beyond repair.

She activated a sensor in her helmet to initiate a diagnostic app for her vital signs then confirmed her weapon remained holstered at her waist. Her sleek, black body suit looked undamaged, and seconds later, the diagnostic confirmed her stats as normal and verified the com-link to her orbiting ship, the *Sif.* She retrieved her gear bag from the wreck and slung it across one shoulder.

Ahead, an endless ocean confronted her. Behind, the abyssal dark of deep jungle awaited. To either side, the pale sand narrowed until it vanished between the two realms. She could swim along the shore or trek through the lush growth to reach the *Mercury.* Either way, she belonged to Nellus now, to its barely charted oceans and inscrutable jungle untouched since its discovery early in the Myriarchy War.

She referenced her frustratingly limited planetary knowledge base. Nellus had claimed seven exploratory expeditions before being ignored because it held no strategic value. The planet's most common fauna, nicknamed *nellies*, resembled, according to their database image, a monstrous mix of lobster and tuna with a long, translucent fin rising from its back. Each had two mouths set vertically parallel and ringed with razor-sharp teeth. They hunted in schools, capable of devouring prey completely in seconds, but feeding frenzies often continued with the school consuming its own, reducing its numbers by as much as one-third before satiating its hunger. Only Nellus's *sea clouds*, enormous creatures larger even than Earth's blue whales, preyed on the nellies. The database listed no such predators on land, making the jungle path far more inviting.

She cycled through her full mission plan. Radiant ghosts of terrain maps slid across her view augmented by meager data—water content, soil composition, weather patterns—regarding Nellus's vast oceans dotted by a few scattered land masses, even the largest of which sometimes vanished beneath its tides. Sarah knew even less about her objective: the abducted girl.

The Commission's need for secrecy rankled her. With all the resources at its disposal, it had sent her on what should have been a simple recovery run—but the Commission never called on Sarah for anything simple. Her direct lineage back to Earth qualified her as a Registered Agent, eligible for the service's highest ranks and the trust that necessitated. She only pulled missions that required exceptionally hard work or exceptionally difficult choices, the kind that could sway the future of the Commission. Even more unusual, Cultural Relations Commissioner Ariana Dey had issued her orders. The lone Commissioner from Darinthe, the only world to stay independent after choosing the wrong side in the Myriarchy War, Dey stood apart from her ruling colleagues despite talk of her secret romance with Pen Bouchard, the First among the Commissioners. The unspoken bonds and tenuous alliances beneath the Commission's surface seemed as daunting as Nellus' oceans, the rumors of fresh dissent as challenging as its jungles. The lost girl could be anyone; her abduction could mean anything.

Sarah locked the homing signal on her display and entered the jungle. The ground rose in shallow steppes as if carved by giants, eroded by rising and falling tides over the course of many centuries. A leafy canopy diminished all but the strongest rays of sunlight, which proved enough to baffle her low-light-enhancement function, forcing her to rely on the spotlight affixed to the side of her helmet. The homing signal pinned the wreck a mile from her position, maybe half an hour's walk through the tangled vegetation.

Clusters of soft, fleshy vines dangled from the trees. When Sarah pulled on them, they snapped and exuded a milky green sap. She gazed above her, seeking their origin, but the dusky heights revealed nothing. Dense vine curtains thickened or parted with the subtlety of wind currents tickling water until Sarah realized they moved with a purpose, directing her toward the jungle's core. Whenever she corrected course, the vines closed ranks and guided her in another direction. She walked a few feet, tried again to turn, eliciting the same response. Now the vines grew stronger and coarser. The pathway they shaped offered a tunnel defined by a loose mesh before it tapered into darkness.

Sarah's spotlight penetrated the shadows. At the light's farthest limit, a huge, indistinct mass recoiled from the artificial brightness.

She slid her knife from its sheath on her thigh and slashed at the forbidding vines. Her blade severed the thinnest ones but only gouged chunks from the largest. Bits of plant matter dropped down and disgorged muddy green ooze. Sarah lashed out and pushed onward, moving as swiftly as she could manage.

Something stirred in lumbering pursuit.

The vines rustled, and the ground quivered—then in a moment, the vines slithered rapidly together to form a swaying wall behind her, broken only where she'd cut them. A menacing bulk trundled along the other side, afraid or unable to pursue Sarah farther. Eager to put distance between her and whatever the vines hid, Sarah resumed her ascent, gripping exposed tree roots and protruding stones until she reached the island's peak. From there, she spied an unexpected and unwelcome sight.

Devastation scarred the hillside. A crater roughly thirty feet in diameter. Rocks and soil, spewed upward by the impact, coated the surrounding turf. Trees lay scattered at the edge of the blast area, letting full sunlight pour into the jungle. Sarah's sensors read the crater as cold, hours old. She saw no sign of the object that had created it. One edge had crumbled in on itself. Loose dirt had then been packed down, forming a crude ramp out of the concavity. Wide patches of trampled soil led up and away like mammoth footprints. Sarah read the signs and identified the likely cause of the crater as a killing machine programmed to camouflage its landing as a meteorite impact, a weapon outlawed after the Myriarchy War, now controlled only by the Commission. The sight chilled her so much she feared she might already have lost any chance of saving the girl.

Chasing the fairy flicker of the homing signal, she raced around the crater, her body suit protecting her against branches and thorns. Pushing faster, she soon reached the shore, sloshing into mud that surrendered to shallow water that frothed as she stampeded into it. She struggled against the current as the surf rose to her knees, then to her waist, then emerged into undiluted daylight. The homing icon flickered. Not far away, the *Mercury*'s dim bulk shimmered underwater.

Her sensors showed no activity in the area. She primed her body suit for submersion, switching from filtered air to internal supply, and then dove beneath the surf. The craft rested twenty-five feet below her. Only a little farther, the shoreline plummeted, the change in depth darkening the liquid vista. As Sarah neared the *Mercury,* a hole three feet round and scored black came into view at the base of the ship's tail, above the engines, most likely the cause of its crash. She swam to the hatch. Her suit struggled to maintain equilibrium as she dove deeper.

Sarah found the external release along the underside of the rim and activated it. A torrent of air bubbled out from within as water flooded the opening. The hatch flipped back against the hull with a muted clang. On the fringe of her sensor range, a mass of small objects appeared. Not waiting for positive identification, she quickly slipped inside the *Mercury*, sealing the hatch behind her.

Automatic systems pumped out the water, allowing Sarah to open the inner door. Four space suits hung along the wall in the next chamber. A door led farther into the craft. The ship's atmosphere remained intact, allowing Sarah to switch back to filters and preserve her internal air supply.

Only auxiliary systems seemed active, leaving Sarah to explore the sleeping machine by the dim glow of emergency lights and harsh brightness of her spotlight. She followed the homing signal to a cabin with an unmade bunk, wall desk, and a chair. A girl's blouse lay draped across the bunk. Squeezing the thermal fabric, Sarah discovered the transmitter sewn within the collar. She tore it loose and swore. The flashing icon vanished from her display. She tucked the useless transmitter into her equipment pack and then explored the remainder of the ship, except for the rearmost section, sealed tight against water taken on through the pierced hull.

In the cockpit, she found the pilot, slumped dead in his seat.

A wound gaped in his side. Pooled blood had grown tacky around him. Maybe the crash had killed the pilot, or he had left the ship and retreated inside to die, fatally wounded by nellies. Or maybe the abducted girl had proved tougher than Sarah expected and fought her captors.

Sarah summoned the flight record on the ship's computer. It listed a crew of two and one passenger, all unidentified, offering hope that the girl had survived and fled with the other crew member. Sarah removed her helmet. Despite the ship's clammy air, it felt good to shake loose her short, blonde hair and rub the base of her neck where the helmet clasp chafed her skin. From a small panel in the helmet, she uncoiled a thin cable. She popped open the command-deck console with her knife, exposing the innards of the ship's computer, then snapped the plug of her helmet cable into a memory interface and downloaded the ship's records.

The transfer completed, Sarah donned her helmet, then retraced her steps, pausing outside the hatch as her sensors swept her surroundings, finding no signs of life. She swam for the island, making it halfway before the mysterious cluster of small objects reappeared, angling toward her. She kicked faster, pulled harder with each stroke, racing for the shallows. The school gained on her with terrifying speed.

When her sensors showed it within visual range, she glanced back, and her stomach sank. Hundreds of nellies approached like a giant whip of teeth lashing the water. She sought a rock or reef for cover, but only barren sand lay between her and the island. A tangle of low jungle growth swayed in the water ahead. She wouldn't reach it in time. Her suit would offer some protection but not enough. She slipped her weapon from its holster and switched off the safety.

As she prepared to fire at her pursuers, her sensors detected a new object—mammoth, so big her gear couldn't measure it, rising from below the sea cliff. Then it appeared, a vast form pouring up from the depths, casting a shadow over her, the *Mercury*, and the nellies, turning the crystalline-bright sea to twilight. A sea cloud. Unexpected calm blossomed in Sarah's mind as though a force outside herself reached out to reassure her. Then the huge creature twisted—or perhaps merely turned a limb—and the school of nellies scattered. Half disappeared in the sea cloud's grip, or maw, or a fold of flesh. Sarah couldn't tell. The others thrashed, struggling to regroup. Exploiting the moment, Sarah pressed forward to the shallows, resisting the urge to look back at the sea cloud until she pulled herself from the water and into the notch of an ancient tree root.

Away from shore, the sea boiled. The partial outline of a behemoth corralled the remaining nellies. Sarah tongue-flicked to snap on her helmet camera then watched the beast roil the ocean, dispersing the school of nellies, consuming those too slow to flee. With a grace that contrasted its bulk, the sea cloud slipped back over the cliff, descending to the onyx deeps. After it left, Sarah shut her eyes and rested.

After she caught her breath, she re-entered the jungle.

She arranged topographical charts on her display, choosing to start at the island's highest point. From there, she would survey the terrain and mark the center of her search, hoping the girl had reached shore and survived. She plotted a route to avoid the area of the vines. Compass readings replaced the maps on her visor.

At the peak of the island, Sarah climbed the tallest tree until her weight threatened to snap the limbs. To the east, the sun fell lazily to the horizon, its reflection setting the sea afire. Sarah's visor magnified her view, allowing close sight of the ground through gaps in tree cover with enough detail to discern the pattern in their bark. Here and there, she recognized the coloring of the vines that had interfered with her earlier. The rustling trees in those places testified to the presence of whatever creature dwelled there. She spied the sea to the west, the water unburdened by reflection, and saw dark shapes sailing below the waves like vast flowing wings. More sea clouds. She scrutinized the island to the last detail, passing over the same stretches of land and leaves until she was certain they held no clues.

Night sped upon her. Sarah puzzled over the girl's absence, fearing her lost in the sea—then, in the western shallows, harsh light glimmered to life beneath the water. Brightening as it neared the surface, it broke into the air like a miniature sun. Sarah magnified and shaded her view until she confirmed her worst fear. A mechanical demon appeared on the shore. Ornamented with heavy weaponry, its brightness blazing stark shadows on the sea, a Cerberus Assassin swiveled then marched onto land. Her scanners detected radiation, indicating a leak in one of its power supplies. It had likely submerged to stave off overheating. She wondered what on Nellus could have hurt it.

Cerberus Assassins, unstoppable by conventional weapons and capable of operating in the vacuum of space, resembled an articulated tank built in humanoid form for psychological intimidation. They bore an arsenal of powerful sensors.

Compartmentalized power sources let any part of the machine carry on despite damage to the rest. The Assassins had hastened the end of the Myriarchy War. Afterward, the Commission—deeming them too dangerous—gathered them together and outlawed them to preserve the tenuous peace.

The machine's glow flickered as it entered the jungle. Sarah marked its progress by the muted light. It gave wide berth to the vine clusters. Sarah extrapolated its route across the terrain. The only unusual feature in the weapon's path was a barren hill of exposed rock, where, almost invisible in the night, a thin column of smoke rose. Switching to thermal sensors revealed a heat source at its base: a fire, either freshly lit or masked from earlier detection by the rim of the hills.

Sarah calculated the distance to find herself closer than the Assassin. She scrambled down the tree, jolted to the ground, then rushed into the jungle, hoping to reach the smoke source first. Heat sensors guided her to the intense infrared blur on her map.

She circled the campsite, her sensors showing only flame, registering only the night sounds of the jungle and the surf's constant drumming. On the edge of the firelight, she wrapped her hand around the grip of her weapon. To one side of the clearing, an opening in a short rock face suggested a cave entrance. A second rock wall rose sheer and high beside it. Footprints marred the smooth dirt—a larger set and a small set. Sarah's heart raced. She peered into the crevasse with her spotlight.

The pocket cave stretched back to a spacious nook. Propped against the far wall rested a corpse in a uniform identical to that of the dead pilot in the *Mercury*'s control room, his head slumped on his chest, eyes open and glassy, hands clutched over a bloody wound in his torso.

A scraping sound from the rock above caught Sarah's attention.

She aimed the spotlight beam at the cliff top. A girl stood there, no older than eleven or twelve, clothes torn, face dirt-smeared, brown hair a tangle around her head. She regarded Sarah with a serious, stubborn expression, her quivering arms lofting a pumpkin-sized stone overhead, the stance of a defiant warrior ready to strike.

"Do what I say, or I'll drop this on your stupid head," the girl said.

"I'm here to help you, kid," Sarah said.

"Drop your gun and walk over by the fire."

"You're wasting time. Put that rock down, and let me help you."

The girl kicked a stone off the cliff. It bounced off Sarah's helmet. "Do what I said!"

"All right, all right." Sarah dimmed the spotlight, lessening the glare in the girl's eyes. She placed her weapon on the sand then walked to the campfire.

The girl followed along the ridge of the rock face. "Now go away."

"Listen, I'm here to rescue you. If I go away, I won't be doing a very good job."

"I don't trust you."

"I'm going to remove my helmet so you can see my face, okay?" Sarah lifted off her helmet, then set it down beside her feet. "See? My name is Sarah. What's yours?"

The girl only stared.

"How much longer do you think you can hold that rock over your head?"

A snap of the girl's wrists sent the rock whistling down, thudding a few feet away from Sarah. She flinched but stood her ground. On the crest of the ridge, the girl vanished.

"I'm coming down." The small voice echoed from behind the wall of the narrow cove. "I recognize you from pictures in my father's office." The girl emerged at the base of the cliff and joined Sarah. The orange firelight softened her haggard appearance. "He said he trusts you."

"You can trust me too." Sarah sat crossed-legged and placed her hands on her knees. "I'm not the only one looking for you, though."

"You mean the robot." The girl shuddered. "It attacked after we left the ship. We ran away from it into the jungle."

"Did the pilot have a weapon?" Sarah said.

"He lost it in the water when those things ..." Tears welled in her eyes. "... when those things bit him."

"The nellies," Sarah said. "How'd you escape the robot? How'd it get damaged?"

"The vine monster hurt it. It walked in there to get in front of us, but it never came out. We heard an explosion later. I thought it was dead."

"No, it only laid low to cool off. It'll be here soon. It detected your fire."

"I was cold. I didn't know what else to do."

"It's okay. You did the right thing. I'm going to signal my ship to launch a jump pod for us. Then all we have to do is keep away from that thing until it arrives. Okay?"

The girl nodded, then sniffled and wiped at her nose with the back of her hand.

"So, you have a name?"

"Annasol."

"Okay, Annasol, let's move."

Sarah retrieved her weapon. She left the fire burning to misdirect the Assassin.

"They said someone would come, but not to take me home. I figured they meant the robot."

"Who said that? The men who took you?"

"Not them." Annasol bit her lip and lowered her eyes. "The ones in the water."

Sarah snapped around. "Someone's in the water?"

"The gliding things. The ones so big you can't even see all of them."

"The sea clouds... *talked* to you?"

"Not regular talking. I just...," Annsaol said, then hesitated before inhaling deeply. "I just knew what they wanted me to know and knew it came from them."

"What else did they tell you?"

"About the war. They knew it would happen and how it would end. And how it will happen again."

"Kid, what are you saying?"

"You don't believe me. The pilot didn't either. They frightened him. Until he died, at least. Then I think they helped him feel a little better, and he believed."

Sarah recalled the rush of confidence and security she experienced before the sea cloud laid into the school of nellies headed for her.

"Annasol, who's your father?"

The girl frowned. "Commissioner Pen Bouchard. I thought you knew him."

Sarah had accepted many missions from Bouchard, First among the Commissioners, architect of the peace that had ended the Myriarchy War. He faced many enemies, even within the Commission itself—and at least one, it seemed, powerful enough to deploy a Cerberus Assassin and bold enough to target his daughter.

"I do. We're good friends. But you and I have just met, haven't we?"

She led Annasol by the hand into the jungle. Sarah transmitted a coded message to the Sif but received no acknowledgment. Atmospheric conditions could obstruct the signal—but more likely, the Assassin's jamming equipment blocked it. She scoured her terrain charts for a safe haven and considered hiding in the *Mercury*, but the Assassin could tear through the hull or simply destroy the entire ship.

Without warning, they broke free of the tree line and found themselves on a scant stretch of beach. Water lapped at their feet. Annasol's chest heaved. Nellus's twin moons gazed down at them in cool, unfeeling stillness. Sarah tongue-flicked her sensors and located the Assassin, now past the cave area and clearly tracing their path.

"I can't summon a jump pod. We're stuck here for now." Sarah met Annasol's eyes. "Will you do what I ask?"

Annasol fought off a frightened expression then nodded. "Okay."

"We have to trick the Assassin into going where the vines hang and hope whatever's in there can damage it again, maybe stop it this time."

Terror swept Annasol's face. "No! Then the vines will get us too!"

"We'll be okay if we're careful. I wandered into them when I arrived here, but I got away. The vines themselves can't hurt us. Only what lives inside them. We won't go in that deep. The hardest part is we're going to have to let the Assassin see us."

Sarah's maps indicated that if they walked straight to the vine cluster, they would cross directly in front of the Assassin. She unholstered her weapon and led the way. Soon they heard the clanking, whirring, buzzing of the death machine, so out of place in the jungle. Its lights broke through the foliage. Sarah waited until she discerned its silhouette, then took aim and fired three shots. The blasts tore through the leafy curtain, striking the Assassin's metal hide. The explosive rounds merely scarred it. Before the blast echo faded, Sarah and Annasol bolted.

The Assassin pursued.

The night flared into brilliance as the machine fired, and a deafening roar erupted.

Shock waves staggered Sarah to one knee, dragging Annasol down.

She lifted the girl and plunged ahead again.

A second blast flared closer, shoving Sarah and Annasol into the air. They sprawled on the ground. Sarah whirled to confront the third blast she knew would follow. Instead, she faced only silence and the jungle gloom. Obscured by smoke and shadow, the Assassin froze. Sarah and Annasol had entered the vines' territory.

Dangling lines already gathered and shifted to form a path that would seem inviting to whatever swam into it when water submerged the island. To succeed, Sarah needed to go down the dark tunnel, but the Assassin seemed unwilling to follow. She debated firing another round at it but feared nothing short of letting the machine glimpse Annasol again would bait it. She didn't think they were fast enough to risk exposing themselves at this range, though. Then the grinding of gears resumed, and the Assassin's arm probed the sheath of vines.

Her hope refreshed, Sarah lifted Annasol, who flinched at her touch, her eyes locked in dread on the Assassin, then jogged along the path. Vines flexed to guide their passage. The Assassin stalked them, its steps slamming the ground. Sarah pushed herself to run harder, faster, until she reached a clearing, across which awaited a massive shape obscured by vines. The Assassin closed. A cannon emerged from its shoulder and swiveled to aim.

Sarah waited another breath and then—clutching Annasol, now shuddering with tears, to her body—leapt to one side of the path as the cannon barrel flamed.

The shell blazed into the clearing then burst, producing an electric ball that spewed a cascade of sparks through the trees. One-handed, Sarah shoved Annasol behind her, training her weapon on the Assassin with her other hand. From the clearing edge, the machine re-aimed. Sarah blasted the thing, her shots only scorching its plating. The telltale whine of energy building up a charge turned Sarah's blood cold. She couldn't protect Annasol from another attack. Then a bulging shape appeared behind the killing machine, looming over the Assassin like a miniature mountain. Fleshy blackness swirled like a gelatinous storm cloud and grasped the mechanical nightmare.

The robot glowed and crackled with energy at the vine monster's touch, then appeared to malfunction. Thick vines, flush with internal fluid, entwined the Assassin like steel cable, broke off its extruded cannon, and crushed its shell. The vines swelled to the width of a tree trunk. The Assassin's energy weapon discharged, but the blast ended in a muted flash. Its upper torso vanished into the vine monster. Small thunders boomed as it unleashed what weaponry it still commanded. Sarah shuddered at the power of the thing. Annasol clutched her, pressed tight to her back like a shield. She and Annasol had been too small to fully rouse the vine thing, unlike the machine, or the sea clouds, upon which Sarah figured it preyed when tides submerged the island. As the Assassin's legs slid deeper into the shadows, Sarah grabbed Annasol and fled.

Outside the vines' territory, the girl clung to Sarah, sobbing against her neck. Sarah brushed her hand through her hair, whispering, "You're okay. We're safe now."

Sarah took them to her ruined glider, where she tucked Annasol into the soft flight couch. Then she removed the outer layer of her upper body suit and wrapped Annasol's shoulders with it to quell her shivering. Tired and hollowed out, Sarah leaned against the hull of the glider. When the tightness in her chest eased, she reached for her transmitter.

"Don't," Annasol said.

Sarah frowned. "Why not? What's wrong?"

"They want to talk to you first."

"Who?"

"The ones in the water."

"The sea clouds can talk?"

"Sort of. You'll see. It won't take long."

Sarah met Annasol's teary gaze then faced the sea, where a shape rose to fill the emptiness. A heartbeat later, it vanished in a myriad flourish of sharp, glowing whitecaps...

... and Sarah *knew*.

The knowledge came in an instant. One moment she was alone in her mind, and the next, everything they wanted her to know crowded out her own thoughts. She jolted from the shock, staggered several steps, and then, lightheaded, propped herself against the glider.

Annasol clambered from the cockpit. "Did you hear them?"

Sarah nodded. Tears welled in her eyes now.

"What did they tell you?"

Screams and fire, people dying in mobs, clawing across each other for a last gasp of life. Pen Bouchard's decapitated body on the floor of the Commission chambers, his head lanced on a pole. A blinding circle of pure light enveloping Earth before it vanished. True darkness falling as suns died. Nellus's oceans evaporating in steaming, radiation-steeped plumes, leaving the sea clouds to shrivel in the sun like beached jellyfish. The beasts in the vines withering and blowing away. Her own death in the vacuum of space, drifting amidst the wreckage of the Sif.

Sarah knew what Nellus knew, secrets hidden during the Myriarchy War, secrets the sea clouds had destroyed past expeditions to hide. Time and distance meant nothing to them. All events occurred simultaneously, the entire universe laid bare before their consciousness, a jealously guarded truth.

"They told me who sent the Assassin," Sarah said. "It was... it was your father."

Annasol's mouth gaped then she punched Sarah's arm. "No, it wasn't. You're lying!"

"They told me what happens if you make it back, and I... I believe them."

Annasol splashed into the surf. She faced the dark sea. It should've made Sarah's choice easier, but her gun filled her hand with venomous, dead weight. The trigger pricked her finger like a fang.

"I can't bring you home, Annasol," she said. "Somehow, your father understood that."

"Why not—?" Annasol spun around. The sight of Sarah's gun aimed at her locked her in place.

"They didn't tell you...?" Sarah said.

Annasol trembled, unable to answer. Renewed tears ran down her cheeks.

"If you return, the war starts over. I don't know exactly how, but you're the catalyst. Your father knows it. So do others. Someone deduced it from what little data was gathered about Nellus— or the lost expeditions here sent back more data than what was reported. Anyone who finds you finds all Nellus represents. That's something people will kill to possess."

"Who? If *who* finds me?" Annasol said.

The gun wavered in Sarah's hand. "I don't... I'm not sure. They didn't say...."

Sarah shifted her gaze toward the sea beyond Annasol. The open water, its ever-rolling waves and unseen currents, its strange ecology and unknown depths. Ever-changing, yet ever-present. A vast mystery, like those lingering in her mind as to who'd abducted Annasol and what they had hoped to accomplish. To hide the girl? To protect her? Why had Arianna Dey sent her after the girl? Had she known about the Assassin? Dey, Bouchard, secrets, and hard choices. A meager seed of hope took root in her mind.

Trembling, Sarah holstered her weapon. The moment she removed her fingers from it, the sense of calm the sea clouds had imparted to her when they saved her from the nellies returned, gently nudging aside her anger, fear, and horror. They had wanted *her* to take the first step, to make the hard choice. She knew that without knowing fully what it meant.

"You'll stay here. The sea clouds will watch over you."

"Don't leave me alone!"

Sarah paused as a new thought unfurled in her mind. "They'll make it so we can always talk to each other. You won't be alone. I don't understand it all. They can't show us everything at once like they see it. That we can see any of it is because they're helping our minds adapt. Wherever I am, I'll never be farther than a thought from you, and you'll have the sea clouds. I promise I'll come back for you as soon as it's safe."

Sarah hugged Annasol. The girl seemed so small and drained in her arms. She hefted her into the glider cockpit and stayed until she fell asleep. Leaving the dozing child, she hiked half a mile along the shore and beckoned a jump pod from the *Sif*. Without the Assassin's interference—or maybe it had been blocked somehow by the sea clouds—the signal patched straight through to the automated system.

Half an hour later, she left Nellus.

Four hours later, she convinced Bouchard and Dey the girl she'd gone to rescue had died on Nellus, her body lost to the sea. She provided the homing transmitter and the *Mercury*'s data as proof and reported the Cerberus Assassin, struggling to hide her rage at Bouchard for sending it after his own daughter. If Bouchard felt any remorse or grief, he betrayed none of it. Six hours later, Sarah talked with Annasol.

She learned the girl's favorite color, blue, that Nellus offered lots of good things to eat if you knew what to look for, and that the sea clouds watched over Annasol when she swam in the ocean. Sarah recalled the visions of war that had played in her mind, fading now, less certain with her increasing distance from Nellus. Her entire life seemed less certain now.

She had traded the trust of her position for the trust of a lost girl and a difficult promise, for prospects of a better future. An endless ocean to one side, an abyssal jungle to the other, and in between a patch of warm, shifting sand upon which she hoped to find firm footing.

THE BLACK BOX

Ensign Randolpha Sanchez stared at Saturn, the planet indifferent and spectral through Titan's immutable atmospheric haze, and fought back tears. Titan Colony Ohio's observation platform afforded a clear view of the Utica Dome wreckage, but she forced herself not to look, fixating instead on the mother planet that filled one-third of the sky. All the colonists had accepted the risks when they left Earth but hoped against reason they would beat the odds. Utica reminded them how swiftly Titan's environment could claim their lives. Across Sanchez's view streaked a plume of ice crystals from the dome's ruptured oxygen banks, the frozen tears of a colony shed to the open sky.

They had lived nearly three years Terran Standard Time without so serious an accident. Now thirty-seven dead, the microbial lab destroyed, and Saturn still hung above them unchanging, uncaring. Its rings appeared utterly still, though Randolpha knew they rotated with an orbital velocity range from the inner rings to the outer of...

She couldn't remember.

Landis would've known. He loved their new home so much; he always knew the things she forgot. She ached to hear his voice and feel his hand on her shoulder, their faces so close their breath mingled as he whispered the answer in her ear.

The new life they meant to live together on this new world, over before it really started.

She lowered her gaze and dared to look.

Bits of Utica's wreckage close to the blown tanks still glowed with fading orange heat fueled by escaping oxygen that froze a moment later. A six-person recovery crew flitted around the debris, protected from temperatures far below zero by winged hot suits. Thermal insulation and micro-nuclear power cores sustained internal heat at 14 degrees Celsius while powering breathing gear that mixed oxygen with nitrogen from the atmosphere. The outfits' glide sleeve wings allowed the workers to leap and fly thanks to Titan's low gravity and dense atmosphere. As they dipped and swooped, gathering parts and equipment into a surface carrier, the dome resembled a broken toy to Sanchez. It helped her to think of it that way, to visualize it abstractly and keep it at arm's length. But only for a moment. Then the truth of her loss—of everyone's loss—avalanched over her until she wished she were down there with Landis, dead to the pain of her grief.

She shuddered, and fresh tears came.

In a few hours, she would leave Titan's surface for the first time since colonial planet fall.

She found comfort in her anticipation.

Mission Analysis, Colonial Xeno Council
February 28, Terran Standard Time

On February 6, 23—, Terran ST, Governor Petrie authorized the launch of the scout ship, *Seeker 2*, from Titan Colony Ohio to investigate the so-called Black Box discovered orbiting Saturn by TCO's chief astronomer and lead intrasolar cosmographer, Dr. Wendy Armitage, who located it via orbital anomalies in the rings. Scheduled to depart on February 7 TST, the mission delayed its launch until February 10 TST following the Utica Dome accident that day and the loss of expedition volunteer Mission Specialist Landis Kozinski (Xenobiology). In hope of rallying the colonists from their tragedy and providing a productive distraction, Governor Petrie issued a call for a replacement volunteer for the reconnoiter team and pushed the launch back only three days. On February 10 TST, a crew of four—Captain Nick Holbrook, Mission Specialist Lee Okahara (Intrasolar Astronomy), Mission Specialist Piotr Atwatunde (Xenogeology), and Ensign Randolpha Sanchez (Engineering)—departed Titan Colony Ohio's spaceport at approximately 17:23 TST and slightly over five days later reached their objective at approximately 19:54 TST. They established orbit in tandem with the Black Box above the central plane of Saturn's middle rings. Initial spectral analysis and visual observation confirmed Dr. Armitage's assessment of the manufactured nature of the object but revealed nothing of its purpose or origin. At 04:37 the next day, Governor Petrie authorized contact with the kilometer-square artifact.

The crew of *Seeker 2* prepared for and executed a difficult space-walk, avoiding contact with nearby objects. Forty-three minutes later, two of the crew touched down on the Black Box.

The sight of the Black Box fulfilled one of Piotr Atwatunde's lifelong desires.

No longer need he wonder if humanity alone occupied the universe, for here before his eyes floated an object singular in all of human history and proof of sentient life superior to that found on Earth. Seen firsthand, it defied Dr. Armitage's description as a "black box." Though its cubic dimensions suggested the shape, its skin appeared light-deflective rather than black. Seen in the close, direct glare of their helmet-mounted lamps, it displayed a dull, shimmering magenta hue. Piotr set down on the surface, and Sanchez arrived a few meters away. Their magnetic boot pads found sufficient iron content to hold them firm. They waited while their sensors scanned the object and delivered initial telemetry to *Seeker 2*.

Piotr took the first step along the surface. He and Sanchez had landed roughly centered on one side, and the edges lay half a kilometer in every direction. Holbrook activated the exterior lights on *Seeker 2*, hanging above them, transforming the murky, smooth surface into a patchwork of magenta tiles, lines, and depressions, all comprised of squares of varying size. Every line Piotr followed formed part of a square, every square part of a larger square. They spied no openings or windows nor any means of propulsion.

"You seeing all this with us?" Piotr said.

"Roger," Holbrook radioed back from *Seeker 2*. "Transmission is clear and relaying to TCO Council HQ."

"It's astounding," Okahara said from the ship. "Fantastic. Truly extraterrestrial."

"Indeed," Piotr said. "It may have been here for thousands of years, maybe more. Where did it come from? Who built it? What does it do? How did it come to be here?"

"Whoa, slow down, Piotr," Okahara said. "We're all wondering the same things. Let's go one step at a time."

"Whatever, Lee," Piotr said. "I left Earth because I believed something better *must* exist. A world and a race without genocide, hate, and war, without rape and corruption, and that only such a unified and consciously moral and compassionate race could muster the will and resource to travel among the stars. This proves me right, no? How does it feel to find proof we're part of an inferior, cockroach species, confined to our own solar system by our ineptitude, too busy killing and devouring one another to ever achieve greatness? It stings, no? But now you can all accept what I already know."

"Stow it, Dr. Atwatunde," Holbrook said. "For all we know, this is a suitcase that bounced off some alien's luggage rack. Get off your soapbox. Focus on the work at hand. Worry about what it all means later."

"Yes, yes, fine," Atwatunde said. "Sanchez and I are moving to the next side."

"Moving with you," Holbrook said.

Seeker 2's navigation rockets burned for seconds, and the ship's lights painted another side of the Black Box, casting Atwatunde's and Sanchez's long shadows across the structure. The pair crossed the square and continued. Servo-cameras on their shoulders recorded everything around them, 360 degrees. Everywhere, they saw only squares within squares. They crested the next edge and explored a new side. More squares appeared in *Seeker 2*'s lights.

"Do you think it's hollow?" Okahara asked. "Our scans for density are inconclusive."

"How would I know, Lee?" Atwatunde said. "Maybe a couple of aliens will pop out and invite us in for tea and show us around."

"Sanchez, you've been awfully quiet. What do you see?" Holbrook said.

"Squares, sir. Everywhere I look, I see squares," Sanchez said.

"Investigate one more side and then return to the ship," Holbrook said. "You're almost at your life-support midpoints."

"Wait! Look there."

Sanchez angled her lights along an array of tiny, equal squares comprising a rectangular patch, a large break in the pattern of the object's skin.

"What is it?" Atwatunde said.

"The only non-square we've seen so far. The material looks different. More ceramic than metal. Or perhaps metal coated with powdered ceramic." Sanchez crouched. "Whoa! Did you see that?"

"What? Where are you looking?" Atwatunde said.

"Watch this."

Sanchez passed her gloved hand over the uniform, square tiles as if testing the heat of its surface. In response, the tiles wavered. Their substance shimmered and drifted along the trail of her fingers. She lowered her hand, and they bowed inward as if pushed down by an invisible ball between her palm and the tiles. She withdrew, and they flattened.

"Astounding," Atwatunde said. "Let me try."

He knelt beside Sanchez and played the trick himself, watching the ripples within the tiles and then flexing their aggregate surface up and down.

"What if I do this?"

He reached down until the flexing tiles parted, exposing a black opening.

Lowering his hand farther widened the opening until his lights exposed a compartment beyond it. Sanchez leaned over and added her lights to his, revealing a magenta room with walls formed of more small tiles.

"It's some kind of door," Atwatunde said.

"Okay, good work," Holbrook said. "Bring yourselves back to *Seeker* 2 so we can make sense of this and confer with the Colonial Council about next steps."

"Roger, Captain, but, ah..." Atwatunde said, "...whatever field controls these tiles seems to have locked on my hand. I can't pull loose."

"Sanchez, help him," Holbrook said.

Sanchez gripped Atwatunde's arm and lent him her strength. "Pull, Piotr!"

"I am pulling. Do you think I am not pulling? Of course, I am pulling! Something's pulling me the other way. What is…?"

Atwatunde pitched forward, dragging Sanchez with him. The tiles curved into a funnel. Atwatunde vanished inside it, and then the tiles sealed themselves tight after him, clamping tight against Sanchez's waist. The tiles crushed her. A crystalline stream of air jetted from her suit. Her scream filled the comms. The tiles reopened, and she sank into the Box, the aperture resealing itself after her.

Mission Analysis Overview, Colonial Xeno Council February 28, Terran Standard Time

Atwatunde reported a force pulling him and Sanchez into a square room with walls made of the same miniature tiles they encountered on the Black Box surface. Radio contact continued for a time, but telemetry failed immediately, as did all exterior sensors on the pair's spacesuits. The tiles had seriously injured Sanchez and compromised her suit. She sealed her suit breach but could not move her legs. Advised by Holbrook and Okahara from the *Seeker 2*, Atwatunde attempted to exit the Box. The interior tiles, though, did not respond to his touch. Within the uniform walls, he soon lost his sense of which of the six surrounding panels had admitted them. Sanchez's damaged suit quickly bled out its remaining life support resources. By the time Atwatunde's systems hit critical, he had made no progress toward freeing himself and remained unsure of the environment within the compartment due to sensor failure.

Holbrook and Okahara attempted a rescue, sending Okahara to the Black Box to activate the opening from the exterior in hopes of freeing her crewmates. Tethered to the *Seeker 2*, she traveled to the object's surface. All communication from Atwatunde and Sanchez ceased at that time, indicating the prospect that Okahara might only recover rather than rescue her crewmates. She found the surface as described: magenta in close light and comprised of an infinite variety of squares. The tiles of the rectangular access point reacted to her presence, but her lights revealed only more tiles on the other side, no sign of her crewmates.

Reviews of Okahara's suit cam recording (files attached) confirm her report.

Seeking her crewmates, Okahara lowered herself into the opening. The tiles closed after her, leaving a gap around the tether line. Inside, Okahara discovered Atwatunde's and Sanchez's spacesuits, floating discarded in the chamber, no other sign of their occupants. She, too, failed to manipulate the inner walls, even when pressing her fingers into the gap around her tether to pull them open. She then requested Holbrook remove her by withdrawing the tether. The force within the Black Box intensified, though, until its opposition to the *Seeker 2* risked impact with the ship. Captain Holbrook's quick disconnection of Okahara's tether and firing all nav engines at full power kept the ship from colliding with the artifact.

He briefly resumed radio contact with Okahara, who acknowledged his correct decision to protect the ship. He then lost contact. Checking her last logged suit telemetry, Holbrook saw Okahara's life support nearly exhausted.

Okahara found the life support resources in Atwatunde's and Sanchez's suits run down to null and Sanchez's irreparably damaged. Nervous, she checked her own reserves and discovered them draining at an alarming rate. Even if she escaped the Black Box, she lacked enough air and power to return to the *Seeker 2*.

Her calls to Holbrook remained unanswered, as if the Box had cut her off.

She prodded the impassive walls, poked around in every corner. If she couldn't leave, she wanted to explore, but the tiles imprisoned her. Everywhere she looked, she saw neat, identical squares, each one built of many smaller squares, which in turn held still smaller squares. She wondered what a microscope would reveal.

Her air grew stale. Alert lights flashed in her helmet.

She gasped for breath. Soon her vision grayed, and cold crept into her.

Her life support had drained impossibly fast, and external sensors failed.

She controlled her breathing and hung on as long as she could.

When pain filled her empty lungs and her chest ached, she said, "The hell with it," and released her helmet to float along with the other discarded gear, surrendering to the instinct to breathe. Instead of the freezing blast she anticipated, soft warmth tickled her face. She gasped and inhaled sweet air. The ache in her chest subsided. Her breathing calmed. Her sight cleared. A sinking feeling gripped her stomach as artificial gravity activated. She dropped alongside the discarded equipment onto a panel of the room. She no longer knew which one in relation to the entrance.

The next moment fire ignited in her skin, and she screamed, batting at herself.

No, not fire, she realized, calming.

Itching.

Every inch of her flesh itched as if a cloud of mosquitoes had fed on her.

She scurried out of her suit, driven by the unbearable irritation of it against her skin, pausing to rub her flesh raw as each piece came off. Soon she stood in her underwear, gear piled around her. The itching subsided. Aside from streaks of red where she'd clawed herself, her skin appeared fine. The sugary taste of the air lingered on her tongue.

She stowed her gear with Atwatunde's and Sanchez's in a corner, then leaned against a wall and closed her eyes.

A screech of static startled her. It pierced her ears for nearly a minute, rising and falling in modulation, a pattern she couldn't decode. When it ended, she shut her eyes once more and fell back against the wall.

The tiles gave way under her weight, and she fell through into an adjoining chamber formed of yet more squares.

The wall closed behind her. She climbed to her feet. Square buttons, meters, and oscillators blinked and jumped on the walls of this new space. A gluey wetness tickled Okahara's bare feet. The square beneath them exuded an oily, amber fluid that rose to her ankles. More sugary air whooshed into the room. A series of deep thuds above her preceded a square panel opening to permit the descent of a shimmering cube formed of the same oil, held in shape by an invisible force. The oil at her feet cemented her in place as the cube—large enough to contain her—lowered, running down her face like warm shampoo. She held her breath as long as she could. When she finally gave out, the syrupy fluid flooded her throat.

The cube completed its descent. Underfoot, the floor panel opened. The gelid prison descended into the Black Box, taking Okahara with it.

Mission Analysis Overview, Colonial Xeno Council
February 28, Terran Standard Time

Holbrook attempted for three hours to reestablish communication with Atwatunde, Okahara, and Sanchez. He observed and recorded the Black Box, which showed no outward signs of activity during that time, and continued steady communications with Council HQ, who advised him to maintain orbit and wait. What occurred in the subsequent hours remains uncertain. Holbrook suffered a memory loss from approximately 16:13 to 19:22 hours. He watched the Black Box from *Seeker 2* up until 16:13—when consciousness returned, he found himself piloting *Seeker 2* back to Titan with Okahara and Sanchez on board. Holbrook has no recollection of how they returned to the ship. His memory resumes with his hands at the *Seeker 2*'s controls, the Black Box already a hundred thousand kilometers distant.

Okahara and Sanchez declined to discuss with him their experiences inside the Box or what had happened to Atwatunde. Sanchez refused to remove Atwatunde's space suit, which she had taken for her return. Holbrook reports they spoke only in whispers to each other for the trip home, isolating him. He felt threatened by the uncertainty and exclusion, by "sidelong glances" in his direction, and a sense of condescension as if they no longer viewed him as their mission leader but as a hired pilot. Okahara seemed most like herself. Sanchez shirked all her duties and spent her time reading and rereading reports from the Utica Dome accident investigation.

Debriefings of Okahara and Sanchez concur: They saw no signs of extraterrestrial life on board. The ship appeared to work automatically, fueled by an unidentified power source.

Okahara posited the Box as an "automatic alien ambulance" that allows injured or sick beings to "fall" inside the "airlock" but contains them until it heals their illness or injury. As a function of the treatment process, the Box interferes with life support, draining it, and forcing entrants from their spacesuits before infusing their bodies with nanite-laden air that reports their biology and health status to the Box's operating system. The burning/itching sensation Okahara experienced, a side effect of the nanites, motivates the patient to remove any gear that could hamper treatment. How the Box might treat incapacitated patients remains unknown.

Okahara suggested the Box's light-absorbent exterior camouflages it at a distance and that the Box may even have caused Holbrook's blackout to conceal its location.

Two members of this council believe Okahara withheld information observed or received inside the Box, although she has cooperated more fully than Sanchez, who has refused to remove Atwatunde's spacesuit since returning to TCO, and, during the Council's entire investigation, has single-mindedly demanded access to Utica Dome, which the Council has refused.

Sanchez confirmed, however, that, consistent with Okahara's experience, both she and Atwatunde "fell" from the airlock into adjoining chambers where cubes formed of an unknown, highly viscous substance contained them and proceeded to "heal" them. She noted that the pain of her injuries vanished the moment the cube made contact with her.

In her debriefing, Okahara described this experience as follows (full transcript attached):

> *Okahara:* Light. Warmth. Flavors—weird, I know, but there they were, salty, sweet, and acidic, like it was cycling through for the one I liked best. It settled on strawberries. Not real ones. The kind used to flavor candy. Artificial strawberry. I've always loved that taste. Light refracted in the fluid and created shimmers, especially bright to my peripheral vision. Inside, the cube was peace-

ful, like watching fireworks too far off to hear the shells burst. The fluid massaged me. It took tissue samples and drew blood right through my skin. First, it studied me to… well, I think to determine what sort of being I am.

Has it ever met a human before? Is our DNA in its memory? It couldn't have been, right? Whoever made the Box would've stocked their own DNA and that of other species they knew, not humans—although we're there now. Considering what it did to Sanchez, I'd say it recognizes multiple forms of life and attempts to find genetic analogs when it encounters a new one. Missing a leg or your skin's burned down to bone? It replaces it with the closest match in its data and improves it if it can. That's what it did to Sanchez, but it repairs everything it identifies as damage, physical and psychological. It not only heals your wounds, it fulfills your needs. To put soldiers right back in battle, better and stronger, more resilient to whatever injured them, readier to focus on their objectives. It heals and enhances.

In later sessions, Okahara divulged that she and Sanchez encountered Atwatunde after the Box released them. It had fully healed Sanchez by this time. The three came together in yet another square chamber where their gear awaited them. She saw no physical alteration in Atwatunde but knew the Box had enhanced him in response to its "diagnosis" because Atwatunde refused to leave. "You know Piotr is so damn cynical," she stated. "The Box gave him what he wanted most, and what he most wanted was to be proven right." As she and Sanchez donned spacesuits, fully recharged by the Box in an unknown manner, their suit cams recorded Atwatunde (videos attached) gesticulating and yelling. The following excerpt represents his state of mind:

Atwatunde: I'm better now. You understand? Better than you, better than anyone else. Yes, yes, I was always better than you all, but the cube made me even more so. You're not fit to lick my shoes now! I must be patient with you like a parent with a feeble-minded child. I'm superior to you all. I never belonged on a planet as primitive as Earth, much less that toxic wasteland, Titan. I belong in the stars, out there, with *them*, on other worlds, better worlds humans will never reach. I've always known the truth in my heart, but I suppressed it out of fear humanity would reject or ostracize and condemn me. I was never meant to be part of you! I only need to prove it to the Healers, and then the Box will take me to the better life I was born to live. I'm never going back to living on that cloud-choked hell of a world. The only good thing ever about Titan was that it wasn't Earth. I'm going to prove myself by healing the colony, healing Earth, healing all of you!

Dr. Armitage's recent observations of the Black Box place Atwatunde's words in an alarming context. She has tracked several changes in the Box's orbit, culminating in steady motion on a trajectory predicted to intersect with Titan within two days as of this writing. This morning, Sanchez removed her spacesuit.

In the ensuing chaos, she injured two council members and several security personnel.

Sanchez slammed her fists against the small tabletop in her quarters.

The council investigators seated across from her jumped.

"Please calm down, ensign," Council Member Isadore Bartlett said.

Beside her, Council Member Takeshi Verde offered a sympathetic expression. "If you'd only talk to us. We want to help you. We want to understand."

"Let me leave. That's all you need to understand," Sanchez said.

"Remove your suit, and we'll do what we can to persuade the council to approve your request," Verde said. "Surely you understand their reluctance since you've told us so little of your experience inside the Box, while Dr. Okahara has been most cooperative."

"Don't trust Okahara."

"Why not?" Bartlett said.

"Let me out," Sanchez said.

Verde shook his head. "Remove your suit. Let us see how the Box affected you."

Tension filled the room for long seconds before Sanchez stood and raised her hands to her helmet. "You know what? Fine. There's no time left for this. I tried. I really did try to do this the right way."

She disengaged her helmet and raised it.

The atmosphere in the room changed as gasses bled from within her suit and mixed with those outside it. Sanchez gasped, struggling to breathe the air with human lungs reduced in size to accommodate new ones the Box had grafted into her. The council members coughed as the filtration system kicked in to correct the shifting nitrogen-oxygen balance.

Sanchez's spacesuit fell away. She stepped out of it and stretched, raising her arms. Fleshy pink membranes pressed flat against her inner arms unraveled from her wrists to armpits and snapped taut. Her coarse and thickened skin scraped and rustled with every move. Five magenta squares, each made of smaller squares, hung from her waist on a belt of square links.

"I'm going to Utica Dome now to heal them. Please don't try to stop me," she said.

Her voice, much deeper than it once had been, resounded in the small room.

Bartlett and Verde recoiled. Sanchez sensed their instinctive disgust at the shock of her transformation. She saw, too, the equal fascination in their eyes, the slow return of control as they formulated questions she had no will to answer. She hated the way they looked at her, hated their repulsion, their curiosity, their excitement at her altered body. She needed the one who'd understand it best. She would hold him again and make him like her.

Together they'd put things right; they'd fix the broken toy.

Sanchez flipped the table at the council members, knocking them both to the floor.

Bartlett screamed for the guards posted outside.

Three burst through the doorway and froze at the sight of Sanchez.

She used their surprise to her advantage, pushing the up-ended table at them, crushing all of them aside, then fleeing. Her new shape and metabolism slowed her down, made her awkward, but no one tried to stop her. They stood rooted to the ground and gaped as she passed them, the squares bouncing at her hips. She made for the nearest airlock and relaxed only once the inner doors sealed behind her and the vents switched on. External air blew in, surrounding her in a haze. She looked at her altered shape, shadowy in the yellowish light, thankful for the mist, grateful it hid her from the peering eyes at the porthole window, that it hid her from herself.

The outer doors opened.

She inhaled deeply, her old lungs closing, her new lungs rejoicing.

The cold barely penetrated her new, tough flesh.

She stepped out, spread her arms, leapt—and flew.

Mission Analysis Overview, Colonial Xeno Council
February 28, Terran Standard Time

This investigation can offer no substantive explanation for Sanchez's altered physiognomy. The attached videos show her active and surviving on Titan's surface without an environmental suit. She flies in the same manner as our winged hot suits, relying on Titan's low gravity and gliding through the dense atmosphere. A security team has monitored her since she exited the colony, keeping a distance to avoid sparking another violent outburst. In the hours since, she has unearthed twenty-eight of thirty-seven corpses from the Utica Dome wreckage and gathered them at the far edge of the ruins. Sub-freezing temperatures appear to have greatly slowed their decomposition, although several of the bodies show signs of grievous injury, limb loss, and decapitation. After completing her efforts, Sanchez removed small cubes from the five strapped to her waist and placed one upon each body. As she depleted her supply, the leftover cubes reconfigured themselves into two smaller cubes at her waist. The dispensed cubes soon enlarged by an unknown means until each one fully contained a single corpse. The magenta sheen of the cubes then faded to amber.

At this time, Dr. Armitage alerted the council to an abrupt increase in the speed of the Black Box, reducing its estimated arrival time from forty-eight hours to twelve.

From the observation deck, the full council watched the shocking occurrences in what remained of Utica Dome. After eleven hours of "incubation time," the amber cubes thinned, grew translucent, and allowed all to see movement inside. Though no one wished to accept it, no other explanation seemed plausible but that the cubes had miraculously reanimated the dead colonists. Over the next hour, the cubes dissipated into Titan's haze, exposing twenty-eight healed colonists, limbs restored, bodies altered in a manner similar to Ensign Sanchez's. Thick-skinned and deformed, they walked openly in Titan's atmosphere. They jumped and glided. For a while, they simply moved, testing and adjusting to their transformed bodies.

They later gathered around Sanchez, who singled out one among them, recognizable as Mission Specialist Landis Kozinski. The two embraced. The others encircled them, reverent in their presence until they parted, and the group then set to salvaging debris, creating makeshift shelters.

At the council's order, the security team approached.

Sanchez, Kozinski, and three others quickly turned them back.

They promised they meant no harm to anyone and would allow them to inspect Utica Dome once they prepared it sufficiently, citing a lack of time before an important event would occur. At this time, the Black Box appeared to the naked eye in Titan's sky, beating out all of Dr. Armitage's estimates. Okahara, who had remained in quarters during these events, advised the Colonial Council to prepare for conflict.

Okahara: That will be Piotr. He's here to destroy us all. I told you the Box healed and enhanced. It rebuilt the wounded to better prepare them to meet their goal. Imagine soldiers focused on a single objective, falling into the box, then emerging better equipped to concentrate and deal with the ever-changing conditions of combat. Your enemy has a secret weapon? One survivor returns to the Box and updates the programming to make all those healed later resistant. Your enemy is physically superior? Not so after the Box fixes you. Your adversary holds an intellectual or psychological advantage? The Box corrects for that as well. It did no less for each of us. But ask yourselves this: What did each of us perceive as our objective or opponent? Because the Box only sees things in terms of conflict. It didn't reveal who made it or how it came here, but that much was very clear. Sanchez wanted to make her life on Titan. Piotr wanted freedom from the limits of his humanity. He overlooked the irony that he received it from a war machine. And, yes, I see your question. What about me? I love humanity, and I love Titan. When Piotr lands, I'm going to take the Box from him and use it to heal everyone and set all humankind free.

The Council ordered a security team to take Okahara into custody. As they approached her, she emitted an unknown form of energy that killed the entire team instantly. Okahara stated their deaths meant nothing because they would be healed and restored once she seized the Box from Atwatunde. She then killed most of the Council to stop them from interfering with her. She did the same to any who opposed her. Only three members of the Council escaped. We complete and transmit our report to Earth in hopes of warning you. The power contained within the Box relates purely to conflict. It heals only to better destroy. We cannot explain its origins or how it came to orbit Saturn. We cannot guess how the conflict about to begin here on Titan will end. Whatever the outcome, Earth must prepare.

Standing atop a shattered wall at Utica Dome, Sanchez watched the Black Box descend through Titan's clouds. Landis joined her, taking her hand in his. Behind them, others of their new kind gathered. Sanchez unleashed an ardent cry that carried deeply through the air.

The Black Box touched down, swirling the yellow haze.

Sanchez leapt and spread her wings. Landis launched at her side.

The others like them followed, each one echoing her defiant call.

The Law of the Kuzzi

The boys hunkered low on the sheet-metal platform and waited for the next chromatic eruption to illuminate the night. They weren't supposed to climb so high up on the narrow catwalk that topped one tower of the New Dodge dew wells. The fragile array of thermal reactive sheeting, strung on hinges between several makeshift framework structures, captured condensation and funneled it into low, squat tanks in the valley below. The settlers had salvaged the sheeting from the *Triumphant*'s massive cooling system, and despite its durability, its reactive coating eventually grew stale with wear. After more than four decades on Byanntia, they had little left unused in storage. Bad enough, the danger for the boys climbing around on the lightweight structures untended in the dark, but lately, the dew wells had proven barely adequate to bolster the community water supply. Damage to even one tower could jeopardize lives.

Such thoughts, though, remained as far from the boys' minds as Byanntia was from Earth. Tonight was a celebration, fireworks the trio had anticipated through months of hard toil and rigorous schooling—ever since Thom Horton and Mick Busco had announced finding the necessary raw materials to make explosives. In each boy's pocket nestled a rare cigar, pilfered with care from the storehouse where they'd spent the past several decades in nulltemp storage, doled out in miserly fashion to celebrate new births and other momentous occasions. Despite some of the farmers' efforts to cultivate tobacco crops, the addictive weed refused to take root in the Byanntian soil. Thus, they could only obtain fresh smoking supplies on the periodic trade vessels from Earth. The next ship, due in two weeks, would replenish the humidor. The boys hoped the new stock would cover the three missing stogies.

Although they knew the importance of the dew well arrays, the boys felt confident that they could come and go without harming them. Not only did the tower offer a secret place where the three friends could savor their booty free of adult interference, it provided the best unobstructed vantage point for the pyrotechnics. Up here, the boys were eye-level with the fireworks.

A screaming whistle sheared the dry air, then went silent while sparks of gold fire scintillated across the black sky. They blotted out the endless twinkling stars above and left afterimages floating in the boys' eyes. The next rocket shrieked upward, producing a palpable concussion and a rainbow of shimmering, metallic flickers. The third turned the world crimson and tangerine and illuminated the landscape like a miniature red sun.

That's when Frank Duncan spotted the long, dark shape trundling over the eastern hills. "Hey," he said, jamming his elbow into Colt Bukowski's ribcage. "You see that?"

"See what?" Colt asked. "Fireworks are damn near burning out my retinas."

"Man, quit griping, already, will you?" Grant Drasinovich said. "It's always something with you."

"We're not even supposed to be up here," Colt said. "We get caught, and you know we're spending the next month digging trenches for the irrigation system overhaul."

"No one's going to find us," Grant said.

Three rockets erupted with a rhythmic crackling, their green-and-amber light painting the air.

"There it is again," Frank said. "Way out there. Up in the hills."

"I don't see anything," Colt answered.

"Wait," Grant said. "I see it. Up on the ridge near that willow sapling, right? Looks like some stray kison calves—oh, damn, I lost them."

"No, not there. Lower." Frank palmed the back of Grant's head and turned it.

"Oh. Coming down the eastern trail. Looks like a Crawler," Grant said. "Is that smoke coming out of it?"

Frank squinted and shielded his eyes with his hand as an electric champagne burst brightened the shadows and thrust the damaged Crawler into stark view. It trundled toward New Dodge. A column of dark smoke wafted from its rear section. The gentle burbling of its motor reached across the plain.

"Who could be out there? Everyone's in the town square for the party," Colt said, now seeing the vehicle. "We better tell your dad about this, Frank."

"Yeah, you're right," Frank said. "Let's go."

"What about the fireworks? And the cigars?" Grant said. "It's probably someone coming in late from Verdi's Plain. Geddy McCarthur herds his kison out that way sometimes, and you know he's always late for town events."

"No way, man. I saw Geddy dipping into the punch with old man Matson before we left." Frank raised an eyebrow and pitched an impatient glare his friend's way. "Besides, that Crawler look like any model you've ever seen before?"

Larger than any of those in New Dodge, the Crawler looked extra heavy, mounted on strong treads with reinforced siding. The boys had seen that much in the tide of light coming from the steady bombardment of cheerful explosions.

Grant shook his head and grunted. "No."

A moment later, the boys scrambled down the latticework toward the dusty earth. They leapt the final four feet to the ground, each rolling to his knees for an instant before they raced off toward the lights and voices of New Dodge.

In the foothills, the Crawler continued its slow progress toward the settlement. Behind it, tall, slender figures crested the ridge, topping the lone, young willow there by several feet. They stood in silent appraisal of what filled the once-empty valley: the building and lights of New Dodge, all of it as alien and unwanted as the short, baldish creatures that dwelled there. They were disturbing, these beings who draped their bodies in patches of cloth and fiber, who worked the land in strange ways, grappling and struggling with it, forcing it to their own ends, rather than living in accord with the natural rhythms. Even the cycle of the Gr'nar, among the most powerful natural forces on Byanntia, had not cowed the obstinacy of these brash and defiant beings called "men" and "women." Tonight would be different. So it had been decided in the hearts and minds of the stealthy watchers. On this night, the frail human parasites would glimpse the soul of Byanntia, and their true measure be revealed.

Far from the darkness of the hills, picnic tables cluttered the town square. The people of New Dodge feasted on fresh kison, whole-grain breads, young stinger leaves, and cakes and pies baked with the meager surplus of sugar, cream, and dried fruit donated by the surrounding ranches and farms. From the walls of the school, the medical center, and the administration building—which most people called "Town Hall"—hung strings of glowing lanterns dripping soft light onto the festivities. A makeshift band of fiddle, guitar, horns, and drums played a fast-paced song that set many party-goers to dancing.

The entire day had been spent this way, given over to eating, drinking, relaxing, and laughing. It was a rare occasion in the hardworking community, one that delivered an invigorating break from work and routine. A true holiday, a fête of distinctly Byanntian nature, different from those times small groups of settlers paid their respects to their origins by observing the holidays they'd carried with them from Earth. This day, this observance, held meaning only on Byanntia and only for the people of New Dodge.

Back on Earth, before the settlers left, before even they built the *Triumphant* and gathered their equipment, charted and planned their journey, uprooted their lives, and cast upon a new course, scientists and researchers had issued an analysis of their chances for survival. It came in the form of a one-hundred-gigabyte document that contained instructions, guidelines, and databases designed to increase their chances of founding a permanent settlement in thirty-seven different environments. Among all that information, a single statistic imprinted itself on the minds of the settlers: the scientifically derived fact that their chances of success rose from 22.7 percent to 64.3 percent if they lasted for eighteenth Byanntian months.

Today marked the forty-first anniversary of the first Turning Point, that historic first day of the settlers' nineteenth month on Byanntia, which had marked a new phase of hope and optimism that carried them through many of the bleak times that had followed in the ensuing decades.

Even the dour Stuart Duncan felt the high spirits electrifying the crowd tonight. At a table near the edge of the square, he craned his neck upward to take in the pyrotechnics display and considered the hardships the people of New Dodge had overcome—the missteps and the close calls, the friends and family members lost and put to rest in the semi-arid soil of their adopted home. He thought, too, of the many laid in the ground for whom this planet embodied the land of their birth, for only those who'd come on the *Triumphant*—the First—could rightly call this place adopted. When they lost one from among the second or third generations, the tragedy always seemed somehow greater than losing a member of the First. Still, they carried on. Each of the settlers shouldered part of the burden, but Stuart felt its pressure more than most in his post as sheriff. He knew good people surrounded him, every one of them, but disagreements were inevitable. Differences of opinion were as common here as on Earth. Such things could poison a place like New Dodge, a town barely past its infancy for all its years on the ground, and, now finally, taking its first steps toward real permanence. Duncan and the town leaders did their best, and so far, it had sufficed. They had guided the town to another Turning Point. But with one weight lifted from his shoulders, Stuart knew others waited in the days ahead.

Sharon Duncan hooked her arm through the crook of her husband's elbow and twined her fingers around his, rubbing their deep calluses. She leaned against him and whispered, "Lighten up, Stu. Relax. It's a party, remember?"

"I am relaxed," he said with a broad smile.

"Uh-uh. I know that look. It's one hundred percent pensive. There's not a slack muscle in your body. So, you listen to me. If anyone here has earned a night off, it's you. It's the Turning Point. You got us here through another year. Now, enjoy it for a couple of hours because tomorrow it's back to business as usual for everyone," Sharon said.

Duncan scooped the back of his wife's head with his broad, thick-knuckled hand and pressed her lips to his, holding her there while the warm breeze caressed them. Breaking away, he said, "You're right, you know."

"Of course, I am, darling," Sharon said. "When was the last time I was wrong?"

Stuart knew the best answer to that question, but the teasing reply dissipated at the sound of a familiar voice calling him—Frankie, hollering from the far edge of town. He turned as his son raced across the outskirts of the buildings, his two best friends hard on his heels, all of them pounding their legs like the Gr'nar breathed down their necks. Stuart shifted around on the picnic bench and waited.

"Bet I know where they've been," he said to Sharon, his expression hardening.

"That boy," Sharon said as her husband's shoulders drew tight beneath her fingers. "Don't let him ruin your night, Stu."

"It's not my night about be ruined," he said.

"Dad!" Frankie yelled again. He stumbled to a stop, skidding to one knee in the dirt, and knelt there panting, trying to speak. "Dad!"

Grant and Cole pattered up behind him, the two boys bending over and sucking air. The run into town had lasted over a mile, but the boys had covered the distance like a sprint, bounding and leaping over rocks and gullies, pumping their legs to maximum speed, ignoring the blood pounding behind their eyes.

"Dad!" Frank said between gasps. "We got company! Someone's driving a Crawler down the east trail. We've never seen it before. It's on fire or something."

"What are you talking about, Frankie?"

"We saw it, Dad, coming this way. A strange Crawler. Smoke coming out of it. Coming down the east trail."

"So, you three were up in the well towers?" Duncan said. "No other way you could see the east trail at night."

Frank grimaced. "Yeah, Dad, yeah, we were. I know we're not supposed to be messing around up there. We just wanted to see the fireworks. But listen, that Crawler we saw will be here soon. You can count on that. It's already inside the shield perimeter."

Frank's quick admission snapped Duncan into focus. Under other circumstances, the boy would have hemmed and hawed, searching for a way to avoid the punishment he knew he deserved for disobeying his father and breaking the law. That Frank owned up without skipping a beat made it clear how much the unfamiliar Crawler alarmed him. Duncan respected that kind of behavior, the kind he'd tried to teach his son, the kind it would take for New Dodge to survive over the long haul.

"All right, I believe you, Frankie. You did the right thing by telling me," Duncan said. "Don't get it into your heads that any of you three are off the hook for being up in the towers, but I appreciate what you've done. Now, listen, I got a job for you. Whoever is coming into town, it's probably best if we go out and meet them halfway. Until we know what we're dealing with, we don't need any diversions. So, I need you three to get down to the south clearing fast as you can and tell Thom and Mick to cut the fireworks short until they hear from me. Got it?"

All three serious-faced boys nodded.

"Then get going!" Duncan shouted.

The trio took off at a dead run toward the town square and the meadow on the far side of New Dodge.

Duncan walked to a neighboring picnic table where the Matsons and the Hughes sat. Jacob Matson and Garris Hughes had broken off talk with their wives, distracted by Duncan's conversation with his son. The last few weeks had proved nerve-wracking for New Dodge as it suffered through its third drought this year, and the two men had watched the arrival of Frank and his friends with worry. The town teetered on the knife's edge of survival, and the settlers despised unwanted intrusions. Bad enough, the skirmishes with the Kuzzi the settlers had weathered a few months back. Up until a bloody episode with the Gr'nar, the Kuzzi had more or less ignored them for years. But after Jacob Matson had single-handedly just about killed the legendary, invisible Byanntian beast that came out of hibernation only every sixty-eight years, the creatures had deposed their leader, the moderate Chief Bollatu, and tensions had flared between natives and newcomers. The conflict had since settled down to a workable coexistence, but it fell a long way from a permanent solution, barely enough to hold the lid on if nothing upset the balance.

Sheriff Duncan watched Jacob Matson rise and felt a pang of guilt, asking the man to exert himself. The lawman and the rancher were both well on in years, but Jacob had recently been diagnosed with a terminal illness and already lasted three or four months beyond Doc Lieber's best expectations. And Jacob had lost his son Chad about fourteen months back, one of the first human victims of the Gr'nar. Chad had meant to take over running Twin Feathers, the Matson's ranch, but that responsibility now fell to his brother, Joseph. Duncan shared his son's report with the two men and their wives.

"So, I need you fellows to raise the Guard. Our better halves can spread word to the crowd to keep it low-key while we set up a blockade out on the east trail. I don't want that Crawler rolling in here until we know who's driving it and why. Bad enough, the damn thing already made it inside shield range," Duncan said.

"Smart thinking, Stu," Matson agreed. "I'll go over to Town Hall, open the weapons vault, and prep some repellers. Want me to sound the alarm?"

"No," Duncan said. "Let's see if we can do this quietly. If it turns out to be nothing, I want folks to have a shot at getting back to the party."

"In that case, I'll round up the men, and we'll meet you on the trail," Hughes said.

Frank nodded and loped off toward the eastern end of town.

Elsewhere, the three boys elbowed their way through the crowd, jostling settlers and stepping on toes. They carved a pathway of surprised yelps and scolding shouts until they broke free on the other side. They flew downhill, letting the incline carry them until each step equaled a bound, covering far more ground than the boys' natural strides. They yelled and waved their arms the whole way. Thom and Mick paused at the sight of the trio, then lit a fresh rocket that blasted overhead, where it unleashed a ring of blue sparks. Mick pointed his lighter toward the fuse of the next round, but Grant plowed into him at full speed, knocking them both into a tumble on grass.

"Grant!" Mick shouted when they stopped rolling. "What the hell's your problem, boy? You trying to kill me?"

Frank explained the situation while Thom helped his partner back to his feet. The two men set aside the next firework shell and squinted into the eastern blackness. Thom raised a pair of field glasses from their strap around his neck and peered through them toward the east.

"Don't like this," Thom said. "Running a Crawler at night without lights is a good way to pitch yourself into a ditch. Must have a good reason for wanting a low profile."

"More likely, it's a bad reason," Mick said. "I told you I saw someone over the ridge past Verdi's plain the other day. There's no call for anyone to be out there this time of year."

"And I told you it must have been Kuzzi," Thom said.

"I know the difference between an eight-foot-tall striped monster and a man," Mick said.

"Whatever it is, I can't say I'm ready to roll out a hearty welcome. Guess we better grab our repellers and hustle our rumps up there with the rest of the Guard," Thom decided.

"You fellas stay here and keep watch on the works," Mick told the boys. "Bad idea to leave them unattended. But don't even think about playing around with them. Need to be a trained professional to do it safely."

"No, you don't. It's easy," Grant said. "Just hold the damn lighter to the fuse, then duck. Hell, you can do it, I can do it."

Mick slapped Grant in the back of the head. "Don't even think about it. Mess with my fireworks, and I will make it my personal obsession to see you on waste-reclamation duty for the rest of your pathetic childhood. I do not need to hear it from your father for the next ten years if you blow yourself to smithereens."

Thom doffed his field glasses and handed them to Frank. "Here, you can hold onto these, too. Was using them to spot our aim. They got night vision."

"Cool, thanks," Frank said.

With that, Thom and Mick dashed up the hill toward the town center.

Already, three men were marching to the eastern edge of town, armed with repellers and bolt throwers. The boys watched their silhouettes cross the steady glow from the lights at the power plant. A larger group of men trailed them, carrying picnic tables, which they turned over on their sides and set in the dirt to form a crude roadblock across the path, about fifty yards outside of town. Next came Garris Hughes and Richard Finch, shuffling along with shoulders bowed under the weight of a heavy noonlight once part of *Triumphant*'s signal array. They planted it beside the tables. Finch swiveled the light's drum around and activated it.

Illumination painted the trail, turning it to afternoon for more than a hundred yards. As far away as they were, the sudden light still hit the boys with a sharp, harsh glare. The rumble of the Crawler drew closer while their eyes adjusted, and by the time they could stare straight on toward the arc of the noonlight, they could see the Crawler rolling across the edge of the shadow and nosing to a stop just inside the range of the light. Black smoke, coarse and oily in the brightness, drifted from the back engine compartment.

"Man, talk about timing," Colt said.

For a tense minute, nothing happened.

Stuart Duncan, Garris Hughes, and Joseph Matson stood thirty or forty feet out in front of the makeshift checkpoint, repeller rifles hanging loose and ready in their hands. The Crawler idled, its engine gurgling and belching forth occasional bulbs of black soot that smelled of burning engine fluid. In the town square, the people of New Dodge grew silent, and the band set down their instruments. The eyes of every settler turned toward the east, where spillover from the noonlight bounced and rippled on the flapping thermal sheeting of the distant dew wells. A stray wind caught some dust from the trail between the men and the Crawler, lifted it, spun it in a miniature cyclone that held for a moment, and then dropped it back to the ground.

With a mighty creak, the forward hatch of the Crawler swung outward, and a man emerged, one hand cupped across his brow to shield against the artificial brightness. He took three steps down the trail then stopped. One hand fumbled inside his coat until it emerged with a pair of desert sungoggles that he donned to protect his eyes. He cleared his throat, and the sound carried through the silence.

"Well, Hiya," he called. "See you brought out the welcoming committee. Not necessary, but much appreciated. My name's Barnes Mungelson. My crew and I apologize for dropping in unannounced, but we could sure use some help."

Mungelson wore loose-fitting clothing of the kind favored by rangers and desert researchers for its comfort and protection from the sudden, swirling sandstorms that plagued the Junsuka. Several days' growth of beard spotted his jaw line. He looked tired, and his left arm shook.

"Always happy to lend a hand to a neighbor," Duncan said. "It's just, well, pretty much every human who lives here on Byanntia happens to be down in the town square tonight. So, I think you can understand our intense *interest* in a new face. What brings you our way?"

"Well, there's damn few humans on this ball of dirt and even less civilized living, that's no lie you're telling. I guess this must be the famous town of New Dodge," Mungelson said.

Duncan's eyes narrowed and he tightened his grip around the stock of his repeller. "Mr. Mungelson, I asked you a question."

Mungelson bristled. "So you did, so you did." He stuck one hand behind his back and waved two fingers toward the Crawler. "Doing research out in the damn desert brings me to Byanntia. Collecting samples, monitoring weather patterns, looking for signs of new and interesting life brings me to Byanntia. Given our current situation, I'd as soon I'd never set foot here. We hit a sinkhole coming across some dunes and slid into some submerged rocks. Banged up the Crawler real well. Our pickup isn't scheduled for another week, but we caught a bead on your satellite beacon and figured you were close enough for us to pull in to make some repairs."

"What outfit you with?" Duncan asked.

"LunaTech," Mungelson said. "Got all our papers and permits in the Crawler. Be happy to show them to you, though I have to say, I wouldn't mind knowing your name first."

"I'm Sheriff Stuart Duncan," he said. "I expect we'll be able to help you fix that Crawler. We got some spare parts and half-a-dozen crack mechanics. I'll take you up on that offer, I think. Let's see those papers, meet your crew, and have a look at your cargo."

"Sure, sure, Sheriff." Mungelson rotated, waving for Duncan to follow him. "Come on with me, and I'll introduce you to my guys. One of them is injured. Sprained his ankle digging the Crawler free. He'll be all right, but I suppose he wouldn't mind some painkillers if you have a doctor in town."

"We do," Duncan said. "We'll see to his injuries as soon as we take care of business."

"All right, then." Mungelson reached up to the hatch and pulled himself into the Crawler.

Duncan looked over his shoulder at Garris Hughes and whispered, "You catch that signal he flashed back to the Crawler?"

"I noticed it," Hughes said.

"All right, then," Duncan said. "Keep us covered. I'm not back in a reasonable amount of time, pull everyone into the square and get ready to blast this bunch to dust and debris if they cross the town line."

Hughes nodded.

Through the field glasses, Frank saw his father's subtle wave, hand at his side, in silent signal to Joseph Matson and Richard Finch. The two men broke off from the group, outside of the range of the noonlight, and disappeared into the darkness. Frank tried to track them, switching the glasses back to night vision, but the plume of smoke flooding out of the Crawler obscured his view.

"I don't believe it!" Colt blurted. "Your dad's going into the Crawler."

"Yeah," Frank said, dangling the field glasses from his neck. "Guess he wants to make sure everything is all right before he lets these people into town."

"You think that's a good idea?" Colt asked. "Going in alone?"

"What do you think they're going to do, Colt? Kidnap him and run? Where would they go? They obviously need our help. It'll be fine. You know my dad. Has to have everything signed on the dotted line before he so much as takes a leak. He's just being careful."

"That Crawler has seen better days, I'll tell you," Grant said. He took the field glasses from Frank and scanned the vehicle. "Look at those scratches and gouges. Must have been some pretty sharp, hard rock to take chunks of metal like that out of it. Back tracks are off alignment. Probably leaking fluids under there, too."

"Well, I figure we can get it fixed for them," Frank said. "As long as we got Choi and Tomlinson around, there's not much mechanical work we can't do."

"You think your dad is going to have our hides for climbing the dew towers?" Grant said. "That was pretty damn stupid, I guess. Not that we hurt anything."

Frank shrugged. "He won't let us off, you know that."

"Look, he's coming out!" Colt said.

Duncan emerged from the cabin of the Crawler. The stranger followed. The two men shook hands in the vehicle's shadow.

Duncan returned to the checkpoint. "They back, yet?" he asked Hughes.

"Nope," Hughes said. "So, what do you make of these guys?"

"Everything seems in order. Got the papers from LunaTech, like he said, notarized by a duly appointed representative of the United Rim. And he showed me a few bins of samples they got stored. Still, something doesn't feel right," Duncan said. "That Crawler has taken a beating, something more than tipping over on some sandy rock, I'd say. And there's a strange smell in there. Faint. Can't place it, but I know I've smelled it before."

"Papers can be forged. Samples can be faked," Hughes said.

"Sure can," Duncan said. "I'm no soil scientist to say whether their rocks and dirt are the genuine article or not."

"Want me to send Pete Dawson to fetch Professor Ridley? He'll tell you in a second if the stuff is genuine," Hughes said.

"Already thought of that," Duncan said. "I see it this way—if they're on the up and up, no problem. If they're not, the sooner they think we're onto them, the sooner this could turn ugly. I think we should get them under control, separate them from that

Crawler, and then we can get down to the nut of this on our terms."

"Why don't we just send them packing?" Hughes said.

"Broken down and injured? They need a place to go. Can't be sure they'll leave if we tell them to. They could just linger around out in the foothills and make trouble for us. Worse, they might find their way into the squatter camp and rile that bunch up. More trouble we don't need. Better to keep them where we can see them," Duncan said. "And, Hell, who knows—maybe they're just who they say they are."

"I kind of doubt it, but all right; we'll clear the trail another sixty yards or so to the vehicle shed. That Crawler ought to be able to make it. I can post fifteen, twenty men to block the path toward the square," Hughes said.

"Do it," Duncan said.

The sheriff approached the Crawler and waited for Mungelson. He surveyed the odd damage to the vehicle, the scratches and dents left as if something had raked across the hard shell and tried to pound its way into the interior. A hairline crack ran through the windshield, and Duncan pondered a dozen scenarios to explain a break in glass fabricated to withstand an avalanche. None of them satisfied him.

Mungelson ambled out of the Crawler and met Duncan at the center of the trail.

"Have your guys follow my men to the garage. We'll get you squared away and see about some food and sleeping quarters for the night," Duncan said.

"That sounds better than fine, Sheriff. I'm grateful to you, my new friend." A toothy smile creased Mungelson's broad face.

"Now, just hold off on all that." A clear, stern voice cut from the darkness beyond the edge of the trail. Joseph Matson and Finch emerged into the light, their repellers up and cocked, one aimed at Mungelson, the other at the Crawler. Something coarse and wet dangled from the crook of Matson's arm and flapped in the half-hearted wind. The men's expressions lit an anxious fire in Duncan's gut.

"Whatever line of bull this scum has been feeding you, Stu, forget it. Him and his men are dirty poachers and liars. There's blood all over the back tracks of this Crawler. We found this in a broken storage compartment back there," Matson said. "Thing is full of them."

He hurled the fresh skin to the ground.

It fluttered in the breeze and unfurled, its blue, black, and gray striping unmistakable, as were the dark red patches of blood spotting it. A caustic odor rose from the dead flesh, the same scent Duncan had sensed in the Crawler, but stronger, an odor he recalled from when men had fought and killed for the right to keep this stretch of ground they called home.

"Kuzzi hide," Duncan said.

Cold dread filled him, then melted away to searing rage.

Duncan swung once, the blow so unexpected and fast that Mungelson took it flat in the center of his face without quite knowing what had hit him. He doped it out seconds later after he had dropped to the ground, rolled once, and came to rest on his back. Duncan lurched over him with his repeller aimed at the poacher's heart. He felt confident his numb knuckles and fingers could still squeeze the trigger.

Back in the clearing, Grant, still watching through the field glasses, cried out, "No way! Your dad just decked the guy, Frankie!"

"Give!" Frank seized the field glasses and raised them to his eyes. "Oh, man, that's a Kuzzi skin on the ground. These guys are hunters!"

"Outlaws," Colt said. "Then that means they're armed."

Looking down at the wounded man, Duncan brimmed with venom. "Give me one good reason not to blast a hole in every single one of you sleazy sons of bitches."

The vengeful edge in his voice shocked his friends as much as it did Mungelson. Hunting Kuzzi was illegal, punishable on Earth by life in psychiatric rehab, but that had not stopped a black market for the creature's hides and organs from springing up. People who measured their souls in wealth and power proved more than willing to spend small fortunes for the pride of owning secret items made of genuine Kuzzi hide, or for the pleasure of consuming the tiny clusters of glands in their chests that contained a rare chemical hallucinogenic to humans. More than enough money changed hands to tempt men like Mungelson, ample lucre to pay for their ships, bribe officials, and purchase equipment needed to land and work in the wilderness. A week's hunt could garner a hundred hides for clever, stealthy hunting parties, though the Kuzzi often proved dangerous prey. Career poachers were a rare breed. One who survived more than four hunts earned the tag of veteran. Those few who lasted six often earned enough to retire and live like kings.

Everyone waited for Mungelson's answer, their attention fixed to the steady black hole at the end of Duncan's repeller. Mungelson wiped blood on his sleeve and cleared his throat.

"They're jes' animals," he slurred. "Not human."

"They're intelligent," Duncan said.

"By whose standards?" Mungelson said. "They're savages. Wild beasts. Dirty creatures roaming the hills with no more sense of social structure than a pride of lions. Sophisticated, yeah, but not like men. Way I heard it, the whole lot of them have just been biding their time waiting to see you killed by the Gr'nar. Yet, here you are, defending them?"

"This is *their* world, not yours," Duncan said. "They're not supposed to be like men. It doesn't mean we're free to murder them."

Mungelson laughed. "It ain't murder, and I really don't care what you have to say. I thought we might work out an arrangement like reasonable, worldly men, Sheriff, but I'm happy to do this the hard and unpleasant way. Now, throw that repeller over here, or I'll have my men lob a blisterbomb into your happy little gathering down the road there."

The top hatch of the Crawler clanked open, and a dirt-matted figure popped up, a broad launch tube poised on his shoulder. The glow of its targeting display colored his face a pale green. He pointed the weapon upward, indicating the arc that would carry its projectile into the town square. Duncan recognized the gun and knew its range, knew what it meant for the settlers. The missile would cover the distance in less than two seconds, then explode twenty or so feet overhead, dispersing a liquid sheet of death to drench anyone below it, burning through clothing to coat their body with thick, caustic oil. Within seconds, the settlers' skin would turn bright red and erupt with plump pustules and heavy blisters. The fumes would travel into their lungs and spark the same process internally. Within a minute, they would fall to the ground, writhing, unable to move, barely able to breathe, then the inflammations and lesions would swell and burst, carrying flesh away in great swaths shed like a snake's skin. In less than three minutes, all those caught in the blast spray would die, reduced to bone and molten meat. Duncan played it out in his head. He thought of Sharon, pictured her body decomposing inside and out while he stood by helpless to save her.

"I got a bead on this prick, Stu," Finch said, steadying his repeller on the man atop the Crawler. "Let me take him out, end this right now."

"Just hold off there, for now, Rich," Duncan said. "Now that we have the truth, I want to hear what Mr. Mungelson really wants."

The satisfied smirk on Mungelson's face burned Duncan, but he saw no option other than to stall until an opportunity presented itself. He activated the safety on his repeller and threw it to the ground. The poacher stood and brushed dirt from his clothes. He sniffled, produced a stained handkerchief, then pressed it to his face, shivering as pain shot through his head and down his neck.

"One hell of a punch you got there, Stu." He groped around for the repeller and found it. "Impressive for an old fart. Any harder, and I'd be breathing out the back of my neck."

"Let's hear it, Mungelson. What do you want?" Duncan said.

The poacher shook his head. "Damn fool you are. You and all your friends here. Trying to find a way to live with those beasts out there while Earth stews in its own filth, suckling at the meager teat of clean meat and produce you send back. Men could take this world, make it *our* world, and live like we were meant to—free! Instead, you choose to scrape and sweat, spill your blood into the soil that drinks it up in a heartbeat like it never even existed. You make me sick, *Stu*."

Mungelson pulled the handkerchief aside, opened his mouth, and stuck two fingers in while he mimed gagging and choking.

"Just tell me what you want," Duncan said.

"Fine." Mungelson drew himself up inches away from the sheriff and leaned in close to his face. "We want protection and shelter until our ship comes to take us away. We want use of your landing facilities. Those miserable Kuzzi are getting smarter. They caught wind of us early this time, and they were waiting. Came at us in a horde while we were stowing our take from one of their hunting parties. Got some new, heavy weapon, battering ram kind of thing, like a redwood trunk. Nearly broke their way into our Crawler, except the thing is built like a tank. We limped away, but they've been following us for two days. Thing is, we can't spend another week exposed in the wild, and we can't risk them interfering when our ride comes. So, you and the rest of New Dodge are going to put us up until then, fix our Crawler, feed us, hide us from the Kuzzi, then help us lift off. Got it?"

"If the Kuzzi have been tracking you, they know you're here," Duncan said. "You're asking me to put New Dodge at risk."

"Understand something, here, Sheriff—New Dodge is already at risk. We used a fair number of blisterbombs fighting off the Kuzzi, but we got more than enough left to deal with your little shithole town here. So, I'm not asking you for anything, Stu. I'm telling you," Mungelson said.

"Think it through, Sheriff," Joseph Matson warned. "Even if we cover these animals for a week and then let them leave, the Kuzzi will know we helped our own kind get away with slaughtering their kind. They'll never trust us after that. Won't matter a bit that it was under duress."

"I know that, Joseph," Duncan said. "What choice have we got?"

"Take a minute to give it some thought, Sheriff. That's all I'm trying to say," Matson continued, and Duncan picked up on the young man's unspoken message—*buy some time.* Something had been set in motion. Duncan did not know what to expect, but he had faith in his friends.

"Go on and let me take the shot, Stu," Finch said. "I'm telling you, I got this bastard dead to rights."

"Yeah, maybe you should," Duncan said, putting on a show of ambivalence. "Figure we don't take our chance now we're delaying the inevitable. We either fight this ragtag pile of kison turds or thousands and thousands of Kuzzi. Maybe we'll get lucky with these losers."

"Uh-uh," Mungelson said. "You listen to me before you do anything rash, Stu, because my associate atop the Crawler is but one member of my crew, armed with the firepower necessary to cripple your little tin-walled Happyland here at the push of a button. Go ahead and kill him. Kill me if you think you're fast enough. You'll be signing death warrants for a lot of people and your own at the same time."

"You're putting me in one hell of a spot here, Mungelson," Duncan said.

"Quit stalling. I ain't got time for shooting the breeze," the poacher said.

Duncan opened his mouth to reply, but the blazing report of a bolt thrower cut him short.

The shot came from the rear of the Crawler, the portion still cloaked in night, and the flash pointed toward town. The poachers had a sniper mounted back there, out of sight, equipped with an infrared viewer and a long-range weapon. Duncan cursed his stupidity for not anticipating such a maneuver as he whirled around and looked for the gunner's mark. A second shot fired. Through the narrow spaces between buildings, the sheriff saw Mick Busco and Thom Horton laid out on the ground at the edge of the town square. Jacob Matson knelt beside them, a pile of discarded repeller rifles at his feet, scattered alongside those dropped by Mick and Thom. Each man carried an armful of weaponry. A small group, led by Doc Lieber, broke off from the gathering and rushed to help the fallen men. Across the distance, Duncan could not tell if they still lived.

Mungelson sneered. "Now, that's about the saddest attempt to fight back I ever did see."

Duncan looked to Joseph Matson and Finch for explanation. Both men's faces paled. The marksman lowered his weapon. "Damn sniper," Finch said.

"I'm sorry, Stu. Dad thought Mick and Thom would get through with the guns, get the crowd spread out to defend the town," Matson said. "We set them up before we reported back to you. Figured it was worth a shot."

Duncan shrugged. "I suppose it was at that."

"Well, what's it gonna be?" Mungelson said. "As if I don't already know."

A knot tightened in Duncan's stomach. Every one of his muscles trembled with the desire to clutch Mungelson and beat him into silence. But he could do nothing. He hated his helplessness. If it had been only his own life at stake, he might have sacrificed it, so long as he could take Mungelson with him. But he had others to watch over and protect.

"Keep your shirt on, Mungelson. I may be ornery, but I know when I'm licked," Duncan said.

Mungelson's face broke into a wide, self-satisfied smile, but it faded fast.

A sanguine howl filled the moonless sky: a long, anguished accusation, answered by other voices joining it in a discordant chorus that rose together and meshed into a single outpouring of pain, injustice, and anger. It thinned the blood of all those who heard it. The tall, dry grass that grew off the trail rustled with movement beyond the range of the electric light. The guttural wailing continued, increasing in volume as it drew closer, and achieved a shrill, painful pitch before it ceased as abruptly as it had begun.

Mungelson seized Duncan by his shirt. "We got no time left! Order your men to protect us. Now!"

Duncan ignored the poacher's frantic pleas. His attention fixated on the lithe form taking shape in the shadows by the rear of the Crawler. The towering figure stepped partway into the realm of the noonlight, where its powerful striped legs identified it as a Kuzzi warrior. The auburn embers of its eyes, still shrouded in darkness, conveyed its disposition. Muscles and sinew twisted and flexed, and a bulky shape flew across the air. A poacher, his hands still wrapped around a bolt thrower, crashed to the dirt. A long spear angled with multiple blades and points protruded from between his shoulders.

A second Kuzzi joined the first, this one taller and stronger, its eyes enflamed with fury, its teeth bared and glowing in the dark. It stamped the dirt beside its wide taloned paws with the haft of its *purjung*, a spear identical to the one embedded in the sniper.

"Must be a hundred of them out there," Finch said.

"More," Matson said.

Guardsmen crouched behind the flimsy protection of the blockade, their weapons raised, their nerves buzzing with anticipation.

"Shoot! Shoot already," Mungelson cried. "What are you waiting for? You'll let them kill us all. Give the order, Sheriff, by the count of three, or I will have my man burn your town to extinction."

Mungelson leveled the repeller toward Duncan and began his count. He never finished it.

At "two," an explosion ripped across the air, followed half a second later by two more. Even the noonlight paled in the sudden flash of colors that bit the men's eyes and turned their movements into strobed pantomimes of activity. In the increased illumination, Duncan saw the ranks of the Kuzzi spread out in semi-circles on each side of the trail, two or three deep in places, their lines stretching into the foothills beyond sight. Their long, creamy fangs, slicked with saliva, protruded from black gums; the dark lips of their muzzles drew back in shallow snarls. Their eyes narrowed to bores of ferocity, and their shiny, black manes stood erect and pointed along the backs of their skulls and down the line of their spines. Each one clasped a twelve-foot *purjung*, arrayed with three or more blades.

There were not a hundred, but hundreds, possibly thousands stretching deep into the foothills, as if the entire Kuzzi nation had turned out in witness for the events of this dark night.

A gunshot cracked. Duncan couldn't tell who'd fired. The clashing glares tricked his vision. A second report snapped. He ducked in fear of stray shots, but no other gun spoke, and he crouched, uncertain whether to run or defend himself. He rubbed his eyes as the particolored flares faded, giving way to the steady clarity of the noonlight. What had happened had taken only seconds.

Mungelson lay sprawled in the trail, blood spattered across his leather tunic, his chest pumping in erratic gasps for breath as consciousness bled from him. The poacher armed with the blisterbomb hung from the hatch of the Crawler, his rocket launcher lost in the dust at the machine's tracks. Half a dozen men from the Guard, further back and away from the full intensity of the explosions, now surrounded and entered the vehicle, taking control from the stunned poachers inside. The men tried to ignore the fierce Kuzzi warriors, who watched and waited.

"You all right, Stuart?" someone asked.

Finch's hand pressed Duncan's shoulder. "Told you I had the bastard dead to rights."

Duncan rubbed his eyes. "So you did."

"Your eyes will recover. One of those fireworks went off right over your head. Another practically set that man on top of the Crawler's hair on fire," Joseph Matson said.

Duncan scanned his men as his vision cleared. He wondered who'd ignited the fireworks. He thought he already had a pretty good idea, but he wasn't quite sure how he felt about it.

The Guardsmen led the poachers from the Crawler and lined them up in a row in front of the vehicle. There were five of them, all dirty and tired-looking, with expressions ranging from frightened to defiant. Duncan felt cold hatred for these men, who were themselves more like beasts than the Kuzzi they hunted. The hum of leathern paws scuffing brown grass and coarse dirt snapped Duncan back to the moment. The Kuzzi tightened their ranks, moving into the light and closing the half-circle they'd formed around the Crawler. Duncan could not fathom their reserve during the brief firefight when they could've swept in and overwhelmed the men with their numbers. He searched their alien expressions, but no face among them divulged a single clue until the tall one he'd noted earlier broke ranks and approached him.

Better than eight feet in height, he loomed over Duncan, a giant of muscle and bone and fur, the kind of beast fit to spawn a thousand legends back on Earth. The Kuzzi nodded and dipped his muzzle in a traditional greeting, then growled a low rumbling sound that rolled on for a full minute. The other Kuzzi echoed him. They stamped the posts of their *purjungs* against the ground, the dull thumping building to a thunderous roar as more and more of them joined in, found a common rhythm, and turned the arid plain into a massive, muted drum that throbbed with fury and heartache. Then Duncan understood their discipline and their purpose. He would never understand how Mungelson or anyone else could consider these creatures less than human.

With all the power they needed to enforce their will at hand, the Kuzzi had chosen to make known their desires then wait to see how their human neighbors acted. Duncan recognized it as a test of the people of New Dodge in more than one way. The standoff with the poachers defused, the Kuzzi laid their claim. The hunters had broken the law, and Duncan knew he could imprison them, hold them until the Rim Authority could send a transport to take them back to Earth to stand trial. But they had transgressed more than Earth law. Didn't the Kuzzi have an even greater right to satisfy their need for justice? The poachers had spilled Kuzzi blood, not human. The people of New Dodge found themselves unwilling players in the eternal conflict between hunter and prey, though Duncan couldn't say for sure precisely which role fit the Kuzzi and which the poachers. Not that it mattered.

The sheriff crouched and retrieved the hide Joseph Matson had thrown to the dirt. He carried it to the Kuzzi leader, cradling it across his forearms, then he knelt and presented the skin as though handing over the corpse of a fallen friend.

"My name is Sheriff Stuart Duncan, and I'm deeply sorry," he said, not knowing if the Kuzzi understood. "I'm sorry for all this, for everything men like these here have done to your kind. That must sound hollow. I know it's no comfort. These are bad men. Outlaws and murderers. We do not associate ourselves with them."

The Kuzzi took the hide and nodded once, a wet rumble rolling in his lungs.

Duncan rose. "I imagine you have ones like them among your own people, ones you single out for punishment. I hope you understand what I'm saying."

He gestured for the men guarding the Crawler to stand down, and as they moved aside, Kuzzi warriors took their place. A line of Kuzzis broke open the Crawler's storage compartments, and then one by one each removed a share of skins and carried away in their arms the remains of their fallen. Soon the lanky warriors stole away into the darkness, the striped furs draped across their shoulders and arms. They moved in silence. Duncan's heart sank at the number of skins reclaimed. He knew, measured in money, they would buy a city, but he couldn't comprehend that kind of bargain.

When the Kuzzi completed their work, the sheriff ordered his men to take the empty Crawler into town and leave the poachers for their new captors. As he turned back to New Dodge, he found Jacob Matson blocking his way, the old man's chest bucking from his jog out from the town square.

"You sure about this, Stuart?" Matson asked. "You remember that day out past Morgan's Bluff, back when we were charting the land? You know the place I mean? Way out on the edge of the frontier? Long time ago, I know, but we were both there. That's what you're sentencing these men to. You prepared to do that?"

Duncan had already considered the sheer rock of the bluff, the gentle, sloping valley beyond it, and the terrible sight it had contained. He and Matson, with ten or twelve other men, had discovered it while scouting the outlying reaches of the region on hovercycles—a thicket of *purjungs* and sharp pikes planted in the earth and draped with the skins and bodies of dead Kuzzi warriors, laid out by a rival tribe that most likely had ambushed them coming south along the bluff. The stink of rotting flesh had been repellant, but even worse were the faces, the flayed skin with eyeholes and muzzles still intact, flapping in the wind from the tips of broken spears.

"I know what it means for them," Duncan said. "I'll never forget what we saw out there, but I'm not the one sentencing them. We're not the ones most wronged by these men. It's the Kuzzi. The fate of these men is up to them. Way it's gotta be, Jacob."

"It was horrible, inhuman," Matson said.

Duncan looked his friend in the eye. Matson recoiled from the stark wetness he saw there. "So is what they did to the Kuzzi."

The Crawler grumbled down the trail toward the vehicle shed. The poachers hollered and swore as half a dozen Kuzzi circled them. They cursed the men for leaving them, but their pleas went wasted. Poking the men with the flat of their spears, the Kuzzi marched them toward the foothills. Soon only Duncan and the Kuzzi leader were left, face-to-face in the middle of the trail, their people withdrawing on both sides, stillness returning to the night.

"I hope neither of us ever meets men like that again," Duncan said.

The Kuzzi leader snarled a low, throaty sound. His fur shimmered as he shifted his shoulders. "So do I," he said in a halting, feral tone. "For your sake as much as ours."

Duncan watched the leader join his tribe. The words filled him with a strange sensation that dulled the edge of his outrage and horror and stoked hope for the future.

When he reached the town square, he found nearly the entire populace of New Dodge circled around a pair of picnic tables on which his son and his two friends stood.

They entertained the crowd with the story of how they lit the fireworks that saved the day; how they tested the wind, measured the fuses, took careful aim, crossed their fingers, and watched the rockets burn. Doc Lieber had reported that Mick and Thom would pull through with some bed rest and careful medical care, and the settlers were already looking to find some humor in the night's events. When the boys finished their tale, Duncan waited for the laughter and cheers to subside before stepping forward.

"Frankie, Grant, Colt," he said. "You boys played a bigger role in what happened here tonight than you know. Maybe one day, you'll look back and understand it for what it was. As the sheriff of New Dodge, I want to extend to you the gratitude of the town for your fast thinking, your bold action, and your good humor through adversity. We might have been lost without it."

The boys beamed with pride, smiles creasing their mouths.

"That doesn't change the fact that you broke the rules when you climbed the dew towers and that you broke them again, not an hour later, when you fooled around with Mick and Thom's fireworks. Starting tomorrow, you're all on three months duty digging trenches for the irrigation system," Duncan said. "And, dammit, I don't want to hear a word of complaint from any one of you the whole time."

Frank and Grant looked stunned. Their grins evaporated. Colt's shoulders slumped in resignation. The people of New Dodge filled the square and the streets of their town with a typhoon of communal laughter.

"But tomorrow isn't here, yet, boys. So, for now, get your butts off those tables, and let's get on with the celebration!" Duncan shouted.

In response, a fiddle played, and a horn blew, and the band picked up a jaunty beat as three young women dragged the boys into the center of the clearing and made them dance. Later that night, while the party wound to a close, the boys, tired and overexcited, puffed their cigars out behind the vehicle shed and grew dizzy on the potent smoke.

Father of War

Kanigher heard the distant dog howl for the fourth straight night.

Its lonely voice filled his mind with a restlessness that kept him awake hours after the other prisoners fell asleep. In the gloom of the bunkhouse, his heart raced, and his head throbbed. Sweat coated him. It soaked through his coarse uniform and into his cot's thin mattress. He had been on the brink of dozing off when the howling stopped. Now the quiet gathered around him, an almost tangible presence held at arm's length only by the sleep sounds of the other prisoners.

Kanigher waited. No more howling came. Its absence troubled him.

Since the first night, he'd heard the dog crying in the dark, its howls had lasted as long as the moon hung in the sky. The lunar glow still fell through the barred, slit windows high on the bunk room's walls, but the animal remained silent.

Maybe something killed it, he thought.

Kanigher sat up, slung his feet to the rough floor, and shivered.

In the bunk above him, Menendez rolled over and mumbled his dead daughter's name. He kept it like a mantra. Everyone in the camp relied on something from the past to carry them through the days.

Kanigher lived on the memories of what he'd accomplished before his capture, the hope that his work had at least saved some of his fellow soldiers' lives. For all he knew, though, the brass had cut his program the day after he went MIA.

He rubbed his eyes, then yanked the blanket off his bunk and draped it over his shoulders, resigning himself to a sleepless night before another day of hard labor in the Pit. It was pointless to care about the dog or why it had stopped howling. The dog roamed free in the ruins outside the walls, where Kanigher most likely would never set foot again. If the animal ever wandered too near the prison camp, the guards would simply kill it for sport.

Yet the howl echoed in his mind. He couldn't let go.

Since he'd first heard it, he'd sensed something familiar in the bestial voice. Something lonely and searching. Something purposeful. A question only Kanigher could answer, though the only answers that occurred to him were impossible ones.

He ran a finger over the old scars along the side of his head and around his eyes. The program, his work, his mission—all that existed only in his past. As much pride as he still took in it, only survival concerned him now, and he'd begun to question the value of even that. Death, at least, would free him from the back-breaking hours in the Pit and his captors' cruel whims. He supposed, though, if he were ready to die, the howling dog wouldn't have so roused his curiosity.

He walked to the end of his three-tiered bunk and, careful not to disturb his sleeping bunkmates, climbed it like a ladder, raising his face to peek out one of the windows. The night stretched into blackness diminished only by the camp lights. He discerned the faint shadows of the tall buildings in the lightless town, rising above the prison walls. In the early days of his imprisonment, he'd seen signs of life out there. The flickers of flashlights or campfires. Evidence of survivors. All gone now. Escaped, perhaps. Or dead from starvation, disease, or exposure. Or killed by soldiers. The enemy still patrolled the empty streets, but a long time had passed since he'd heard sounds of combat from outside the wall or seen air patrols fly over them. The town seemed so quiet he figured the entire region stood behind enemy lines now.

He descended the bed frame and returned to his bunk.

Outside the bunkhouse's single exit, something scratched.

Kanigher froze.

His gaze darted to the locked door.

The low scratching noise repeated itself, persistent.

Skritch, skritch, skritch.

A faint huff of breath came. Then a muffled grunt.

Kanigher glanced at the other prisoners. Exhausted from eighteen-hour shifts in the Pit, none of them stirred.

The scratching grew louder.

Skritch, skritch, skritch.

Kanigher crept to the door. He stepped to the right, crouched with his back against the wall, and listened. The guards sometimes carried out random night raids, rousting prisoners and beating them. Kanigher had experienced his share of them, though, and unlike this, those attacks happened fast, the guards bursting through the door, shouting, flashing bright lights, waving guns and batons.

The scratching paused. Something clinked.

A small beep and a hiss sounded. A line of light appeared in the door, ran several inches up from the ground, two-thirds of the way across, and then back to the ground, tracing a crude half-oval. The glow flared for a second before the thick section of steel door dropped inward, sliced by a strip of quick-burning acid-flash tape. The piece thumped the floor, trailing wisps of smoke.

Kanigher recoiled, shedding his blanket, bracing himself.

His pulse thundered in his skull.

A shape emerged through the crude opening.

Slender white paws appeared.

A compact, whiskered face with tall, black ears came after them.

The animal wriggled on all fours into the bunkhouse, then stared at Kanigher, panting, its tongue hanging out.

Traumatic dementia. First, you imagine dogs howling. Then you hallucinate dogs crawling under doors. A textbook breakdown.

Other prisoners had snapped, talking to invisible people, running from demons only they understood. Inevitably, the guards took them to the infirmary. None ever returned.

Kanigher blinked, wishing the little dog away.

Instead, it pressed its whiskered muzzle against his hand and licked his palm. Warm and wet. Its tongue soft. And the smell of the dog—Kanigher couldn't deny the distinct reality of its scent.

Or its body heat. Sensations so familiar and wonderful yet so long denied him. They set his heart racing. He stifled a gasp and tried to make sense of the little, black-and-white animal sitting by him, licking his hand. A Boston Terrier. Athletic, barrel-chested, large for its breed. Not a dog he'd have chosen for his work but an intelligent, willful, and loyal breed, and with genetic enhancement, capable enough for the right missions. A harness rigged with miniaturized equipment hugged its body. A cyber-cowl covered a quarter of its face, interlaced with goggles that shielded its protruding eyes. Kanigher read the dog tag dangling from its collar: Bug Eye.

The dog licked Kanigher's hand three more times, then sat in an attention pose and stared at him, its mouth hanging open in a dog smile.

Kanigher stared back at it.

The dog lifted a paw and tapped his hand.

Still skeptical, Kanigher studied the familiar gear strapped to the dog's body. It included a small nozzle with cartridges for spitting out strips of flash-acid tape, which had been used to cut the hole in the door, as well as several small pouches along the dog's back, arranged in a configuration Kanigher knew so well he didn't hesitate popping one open and pulling out a tiny square cookie. He gave it to the dog, which ate it, then circled around and presented Kanigher with a tool strapped to its side. A low-level laser torch, powerful enough to cut the lock on the door.

Kanigher reached for it, then stopped.

The dog's presence made no sense, especially not equipped with the rig he wore.

A rig and gear *Kanigher* had designed years ago.

Although streamlined and refined, the equipment remained recognizably his.

He had to be imagining it, dreaming, sleepwalking, or...

The saliva drying on his hand felt so real.

The dog's scent.

Its warmth.

The howling...

Not this dog's. But seeing his rig, the familiarity of the howling dog's voice haunted Kanigher even more. He refused to let the thought forming in his mind complete itself, unwilling to risk entertaining something so improbable. He scratched the Boston between his ears, and the dog lowered its head, enjoying the attention for a moment. Then it snapped back to position and tapped Kanigher's hand with its paw again.

Kanigher took the laser torch from its clip.

The dog retreated to the door and waited for Kanigher.

Kanigher didn't move. The dog wriggled out through the opening, then poked its front paws and head back in and gave an exasperated huff.

Kanigher glanced at his fellow prisoners, none of whom stirred.

Positioning his body to conceal the light, he activated the torch and cut the lock from the door, catching the handle as it fell and then setting it silently on the floor.

The door swung open, and Kanigher stepped outside onto the edge of a familiar dirt path he'd never before set foot upon at night. The camp felt like a graveyard, the squat silhouettes of the other bunkhouses like grave markers. Kanigher searched for guards and spied them on the far side of the yard on the wall and in their towers, rifles poking over their shoulders. For years, he'd gone nowhere, done nothing without them watching him, ordering him, threatening him. The tiny freedom of being outside without permission almost paralyzed him.

Bug Eye took off to the left, then waited for Kanigher, who stood still, overwhelmed by the vastness of the night. Running back, the dog jumped up and hit Kanigher's thigh with its front paws, jolting him. It settled on all fours, huffed, then darted off again.

Gripping the laser torch for use as a weapon, Kanigher followed.

Bug Eye led him along a winding path that skirted the camp's lights, guiding him, step by step, closer to the eastern wall. Along the way, they passed the wrecks of the camp's standard-issue hover-eyes, taken out before they could sound an alarm. As they neared the wall, Kanigher spied a faintly glowing hole in the steel barrier. It looked wide enough for him to fit through if he squeezed his shoulders together. No simple laser torch had sliced through the foot-thick wall, though, which meant someone with heavy equipment and stealth tech had sent in the Boston.

A sweeping spotlight crossed the path ahead of them. Bug Eye stopped, and Kanigher hunkered down and waited for the light to pass before continuing. He considered going back for the others in his bunkhouse, but it would only heighten his risk of capture and endanger them since he had no idea what awaited him outside the wall.

As they resumed their approach, the light swung back and flared on them twenty yards from the hole. Kanigher lost sight of the Boston in the blinding brightness.

Harsh voices shouted in Chinese. An alarm screeched.

Instinctively, Kanigher dropped to a crouch.

A gunshot cracked, sounding like thunder. Another round hissed through the air in front of him. He fired the laser torch blind and heard someone scream in pain. When his eyes adjusted, he saw guards scrambling atop the walls, aiming rifles at him, and guards on the ground running in his direction. A searing, fiery brightness came then with an enraged roar and concussion that knocked Kanigher to the ground and jolted the laser torch from his hand. Gunfire followed, dim in his ringing ears. Kanigher scrambled to his feet, disoriented, clueless as to where to run.

Teeth dug into his hand, biting firmly but not hard enough to break his skin.

Warm breath. Hot saliva running onto his wrist.

A dog's mouth.

Too large for the Boston.

It tugged on Kanigher until he moved with it, and then it let go of his hand and picked up speed, forcing Kanigher to jog. He stumbled on the rough ground but kept moving after the dog. A brown-and-black Belgian Malinois, it wore a different version of Kanigher's cybercowl, fitted above its left ear and eye. Its harness held pouches like those on the Boston's, but the largest bore a red cross in a white circle.

Another explosion quaked the night.

Kanigher crouched and covered his head with his arms.

Muffled screams and shouts filled his aching ears as the thunder faded. Some in Chinese, some in English. *The other prisoners.* The explosions must have panicked them awake, and he'd left his bunkhouse door open. He hoped none of them were hurt.

A fourth explosion erupted much closer than the others. Shrapnel sliced Kanigher's forehead, and the blast pushed him forward, driving him through the hole in the wall behind the running Belgian. Blood in his eyes, he fled the chaos at the camp and trailed his guide down a darkened street littered with burned-out cars and debris from the bombed buildings. His head throbbed. He wiped the blood from his eyes, trying to clear his sight. Kanigher struggled to keep up with the trotting Belgian. Bug Eye ran beside it, the two dogs stopping at regular intervals to sense the night and pick a safe path through the maze of streets.

Kanigher recognized the pattern.

Run five to ten yards. Stop. Scent, listen, look. Then another five to ten yards.

Stop and go.

A system he'd invented and perfected in years of training soldier dogs.

He intended it for safe, fast movement over unknown terrain.

Although he'd field-tested it, he'd never had an opportunity to see it in action.

He kept within one yard of the Belgian. They turned the corner down a new street, and Kanigher glanced back at the fire rising from the camp. A pillar of smoke drifted above the wall. The voices and gunfire faded. Soon patrols would prowl the city. Someone had blasted the camp to cover his escape, but in the din and flash of combat, Kanigher hadn't seen who. He hoped—whoever they were—they were well hidden and had an escape route.

The dogs led Kanigher along a desolate side street cluttered with trash, broken bricks, and cracked cement. The Boston scurried down the block then sat, facing the intersection, watching. The Belgian circled back to Kanigher and lowered to a down position. Kanigher knelt and scratched the dog between the ears.

Kanigher read its tags: Nightingale.

"Good girl," he said.

The Belgian wagged its tail.

Kanigher opened the First Aid pouch on the dog's back, took out an antiseptic wipe and a tube of liquid skin. He cleaned and dressed his wound to stop the blood from flowing into his eyes. In another pouch, he found a stash of cookies and gave the Belgian two. The dog gobbled them, then snapped back onto its feet, curled away from Kanigher, and ran down the street, Bug Eye beside it. Kanigher hurried after them.

They raced through the empty town. Sharp rubble dug into Kanigher's feet, shredding his flimsy prison sandals, but he ignored the pain and pushed himself to keep up. The dogs sniffed out their trail, winding a path east toward the edge of town. They passed the looming shape of a ballistic personnel carrier, five stories tall and embedded in the earth, one of the secret weapons that had enabled the enemy invasion. Then they rounded a corner and came to a plaza outside an office building. A headless statue on a cracked pedestal loomed over them. The building's demolished upper floors threw down jagged lunar shadows.

The sound of distant engines grumbled, echoing off the old buildings as soldiers launched pursuit. Kanigher resisted the panic brewing in his gut. They had put a fair distance between them and the prison camp, but jeeps, tanks, and hoverbirds would overtake them if they remained in the open. Kanigher scanned the area for hiding places. The office building appeared far too damaged and unstable, and piles of rubble clogged the entrances to all the other structures in sight.

The dogs stood side by side, ears pricked up.

Waiting.

Seconds ticked away.

The motor sounds grew and spread out from the prison camp.

The rhythm of hoverbird blades picked up and cut the night.

Kanigher's heart pounded in his chest. He knelt by the dogs, trusting them, knowing they saw a different darkness than he did, and heard a greater range of night sounds. A single, sharp bark came, and then the dogs took off running.

"Wait for me!" Kanigher cried.

He rushed after them, struggling to keep his balance on the litter-strewn street. The dogs raced around the damaged office building, along a side street, then down an alley. Kanigher chased them, ignoring his tightening fear as the alley sloped down into a darkness that swallowed the dogs and left him blind. He slowed, picking his way carefully through debris. Ahead of him, the dogs sniffed and panted. Their nails scratched concrete and jostled rubble.

Kanigher's foot struck a wall. He stopped.

The noise of hoverbird engines buzzed.

"Where are you?" he whispered.

He clicked his tongue twice, a standard signal he'd used with his dogs. A low blue light appeared. It painted an aura around the silhouettes of Bug Eye and Nightingale and revealed a third dog, a Doberman Pinscher, also rigged with a harness and cybercowl based on Kanigher's design. The light glowed from its collar. The three dogs surrounded Kanigher and ushered him through a narrow opening at the end of the alley into a tunnel. They walked for several minutes. The motor sounds died away. Kanigher caught his breath. Soon the yellow-white glow of a field lantern appeared up ahead, pouring out of a doorway. When they reached it, the Doberman sat beside the door like a sentry. The Boston and the Belgian entered the room. Kanigher inched his way to the opening and peeked inside.

An American soldier sat across the room, her back against the wall, head slumped onto her chest. Blood stained her uniform. She seemed very still, but her torso rose and fell with her breath. A fourth dog, a Chocolate Lab, lay beside her, its head on her leg. Blood spotted its fur. Its cybercowl covered nearly a third of its head, encompassing one ear and both its eyes, and it too wore a harness like the other canines. Bug Eye and Nightingale sat by the soldier's sides. Kanigher approached the woman. All three dogs tracked him, ready to attack if he made a move to harm her. Slowly, he took the woman's hand and pressed two fingers against her wrist, feeling her weak pulse.

The soldier kicked her leg, shuddered, and then snapped up her head. "Who's there?"

The Lab lifted its head, bared its teeth, and growled at Kanigher.

Kanigher rocked back on his heels. The woman removed her helmet and tucked it onto her lap. A partial cybercowl covered her left temple and ear and encircled half of her left eye. In the poor light of the field lantern, she looked ghostly from blood loss. Her eyes locked on Kanigher's.

She stroked the Lab's neck. "Easy, girl."

The Lab stopped growling.

Kanigher read the woman's nameplate and rank insignia. "Are you badly hurt, Lieutenant Haney?"

Haney squinted, eyeing Kanigher's face. She reached into a pocket on her sleeve, pulled out a mobile intelligence data unit, and tapped on the screen. The glow lit her eyes. An image resolved onscreen. She held it up to Kanigher, comparing his face to the face of a man in the picture, awaiting confirmation from a facial recognition scan. Though he hadn't seen it in years, Kanigher knew the photo: outside his old kennel and training facility, a red bandanna in his hand, he knelt beside a German Shepherd, Sarge. A good dog. The first Kanigher had put through his cybernetics program. Involuntarily, he touched the old scars in the side of his head where his cybercowl had been mounted when he handled Sarge. Enemy soldiers had ripped it from him when they took him prisoner. In the picture, he didn't yet have the cowl. He looked fifty pounds heavier, his hair clean of the gray that shot through it now, his face smooth and unmarred by scars and bruises—and he smiled.

"Captain Kanigher?" Haney asked. "Is that really you?"

Kanigher read the doubt in her eyes, and, in an odd way, he shared it.

He must have seemed to her like a ghost risen from the grave. He certainly felt like one. She knew his name, who he'd been, but he couldn't say for sure he was still that same man in the picture anymore. He opened his mouth to answer, but no words came.

Haney pulled herself up higher against the wall. "Wow. I can't believe we found you." She coughed lightly after speaking.

"How bad is it?" Kanigher said.

Haney mustered a false grin. "Could be a lot worse, could be a lot better."

"Let me see."

Haney nodded, then rolled her stained uniform shirt up to her left armpit, exposing the bloody wound in her side. She had field-dressed it, cleaned it, then sealed it with liquid skin, but several nasty slivers of metal still poked out from her flesh, letting blood dribble out around them, slowly bleeding her to death. Kanigher recognized the projectiles. Needles from a hover mine. Each a foot long and embedded deep in Haney's side. At least she'd left them in. If she'd removed them, barbs on the ends would've ripped out her insides. He guessed she had a fifty-fifty chance of survival without immediate medical care.

"What's the prognosis, doc?" Haney asked.

"Like you said. Could be better."

"Story of my friggin' life."

Kanigher leaned back on his heels as Haney lowered her shirt. "You need a doctor to stop the bleeding."

"Roger that. Soon as the rest of the squad returns, we can bug out. We get fifteen klicks out of town, and we can call for air evac. They won't come any closer. Too dangerous, especially now we've stirred up the hornet's nest out there."

"Can you walk fifteen klicks?"

"Got no choice," Haney said. "Move it or lose it."

Kanigher nodded. A quiet moment passed, and he sensed the dogs watching him, protective of Haney but signaling something more with their stare. Something like—affection? Admiration? He recalled the plaintive howling of the unknown dog, how it had seemed meant for him.

"Lieutenant," Kanigher asked. "How'd you wind up here?"

"Ran into trouble about seven klicks east of town. An old battlefield, full of leftover live ordnance. The dogs did great. Led us across most of it safe and sound, but the mine that got me sat in the crook of a tree branch. Its hover unit had died god knows how long ago. No sound, no scent for the dogs to pick up on, but as soon as I blipped its proximity sensor—*wham*! Knocked me and Sallygirl on our asses and gave us a good sting. My second, Sergeant Andru, wasn't so lucky. Seven needles in his neck and head. Didn't make it out of the field."

"I'm sorry," Kanigher said.

"He was a good man."

Haney stroked the back of the Lab's neck then gestured for Kanigher to check the dog's side. Five needles, twins of those embedded in Haney, protruded from between Sallygirl's ribs.

"Sallygirl got it worse than me." Haney's voice turned shaky and clipped. "She's the only reason I'm still alive. She jumped in front of me, took the worst of what came our way."

"Sallygirl's a good girl," Kanigher said. At that, Sallygirl raised her head a few inches, met Kanigher's eyes for a moment, then settled down again on Haney's leg. "What I meant was why are you here in the first place? This place, town. Behind enemy lines."

Haney scrunched her face. "Damn, Cap, isn't it obvious? We came for you."

Kanigher shook his head. "No, no. Bullshit. I'm not worth you and Sallygirl sitting here with those needles in your sides or Sergeant Andru's life. Not after all this time. A hundred other soldiers in that camp are worth more than I am."

"Not to my squad," Haney said.

"Your squad?"

"Guess I should introduce you." Haney gestured to the Boston. "You've already met the little guy, Bug Eye. His size comes in handy, and he's got more determination than most soldiers I know. He can get in and out of anywhere if you give him the right scents. And Nightingale you met. She's our scout. Carries our med gear too. Outside the door, there is Marshmallow Soldier. As fierce as he looks, but he goes soft the second you give him anything sweet. There's not an explosive he can't sniff out, no matter how well hidden. Sallygirl is our tracker. The rest ought to be here soon. I feel them nearby."

Kanigher touched his forehead, indicating where Haney wore her cowl.

"Yep," Haney said. "Plugged in and ready to play. I guess you'd know all about that."

"It's been a while. I imagine it's different now."

"The tech, yeah, a little. We get and send clearer sensory and emotional impressions than your original equipment, but it's still only impressions. Thing is, dogs are dogs. They're smart, and, you treat 'em right, you got friends for life."

Kanigher nodded. "I worried all this went away with me."

"Almost did. A year after you were captured, the brass tried to shut it down. One of my squad convinced General Kubert your program was worth funding. They hired new geniuses to continue your work. They're adapting your cybernetics work for human/machine interfaces now. Making good progress too. Rumors about top-secret programs and new kinds of weapons. Hasn't ended the war yet, but it lets us hit a whole lot harder."

"How... how bad is it?"

"Like me. Could be a whole lot worse, could be a whole lot better," Haney said. "The Coalition occupies four states. Used to be six. We're in one of the occupied ones."

"They dropped you behind enemy lines to rescue me?"

"My squad only works behind enemy lines. Guerilla warfare. Hit-and-run. Us and a few other squads spread throughout the occupied territory. We drive the Coalition nuts, fouling up their supply lines, screwing their communications, spoiling their food. You name it, we gremlin it. I've been deployed almost a year straight now, and they still haven't quite figured out what the hell keeps hitting them."

"Are we winning?"

"That call's way above my pay grade," Haney said. "Every day seems the same to me. Cloudy, with a chance of explosions and gunfire. Coalition is dug in deep from Providence to Atlantic City and over to Pittsburgh, but we stopped them advancing past Pennsylvania, even pushed them back a good way. Two years now, we've had troops on the ground in China and Russia to busy them on their own turf. Mexico's on fire, and the border is a no-man's land, but they never did get a foothold in Texas. We kept them out of the Northwest too. Our allies are propping us up best they can, but they've got their hands full with their own fights. At least no one's gone nuclear, yet so that's considered a plus. But it's going to be a long war."

The news stunned Kanigher. "We'd been fighting five years when they captured me. How long have I...?"

"You don't know?"

Kanigher shook his head.

"Guess it all blends together, the beatings, the hard labor, the lousy food—kind of like being in the infantry," Haney said. "Hard to keep track when you're living like that."

"Hey," Kanigher whispered. "How long?"

"Eight years." Haney rubbed Sallygirl's head while Kanigher absorbed her answer.

"Guess I should've known," he said.

Bug Eye and Nightingale jolted to all fours, eyes and ears alert. Sallygirl lifted her head, and from the corridor, Marshmallow Solider growled. Seconds later, a tremor ran through the ground. Kanigher put a hand down to brace himself until the rumble ended.

"Tanks," Kanigher said. "Looking for us."

"No doubt about it," Haney said. "Probably backed up by hoverbirds and foot patrols."

"If we stay here, they'll find us," he said. "The rest of your squad may never reach us."

Haney shook her head. "Don't worry. Those Coalition bastards can't always go where my squad can go. That's what makes us so effective."

In the corridor, Marshmallow Soldier filled the doorway. His blue light flashed three times, darkened, then flashed three more. The click-clack of nails on cement and the scrape of metal echoed down the tunnel. The Doberman backed into the room. Two shapes followed him and moved into the light, a pair of German Shepherds. One, young and lithe, wore a standard harness rig and cybercowl, which wrapped the right side of its head. The second stood taller than the other dogs. It took Kanigher several seconds to accept what he saw, but he knew the moment the dog moved into the light this one had made the howl. Impossible as it seemed, he knew its face and its stance. He knew its scent. He remembered the sound of its voice.

The Shepherd made eye contact.

Sarge.

Kanigher wasted no time doubting it. The red bandanna from the photo, now faded and pocked with holes, encircled its neck. The first of the cyberdogs he'd created and trained, older and scarred, gray in the fur around his muzzle, a chunk missing from one of its ears, and yet still possessed of the same warm, intelligent eyes he remembered. He offered Sarge his hand. The dog sniffed, then licked it, then Kanigher knelt and let the dog lash his face with its tongue and press its muzzle against his neck. Kanigher stroked it and scratched its sides. He felt as much steel under his fingers as he did hair and muscle. He backed off for a better look. Cybernetics and prosthetics comprised nearly a third of Sarge's body, including his rear legs and part of his torso, no doubt increasing his strength and speed far beyond his original abilities. His cybercowl masked the left half of his face. His rig, larger and more complex than all the others, integrated into his body cybernetics, bore a launcher for high-yield mini-mortars—bombs the size of cherries—and a compact projected-energy gun. The weapons used in the breakout. He glanced at the other Shepherd, who wore only a standard cybercowl and a similar rig mounted only with an energy gun.

"Sarge has been looking for you a long time," Haney said.

"I can't believe he's still alive," Kanigher said.

"Around the time the brass tried to shutter your program, Sarge ran with a platoon in Oregon doing explosives detection. He caught wind of an underground encampment, enemy tunnels, an ambush waiting to happen. Saved hundreds of lives, including General Kubert's nephew. Even got wounded in the firefight. After that, the lab boys put new gear to the test on him first, and he made everything they threw at him work. They say it was like he was trying to make you proud. I had my doubts when I got assigned as his handler, but he wiped them out fast. Caught your scent a year ago, and he hasn't let it go. He made sure the rest of the squad knew it too. Like he was worried you might be forgotten if something happened to him. He isn't getting any younger, and this is probably his last tour. Now or never. Him and all the others, they're like your children. You and Sarge set the course for them, for all of us. You gave us a lifeline."

"I heard him howling," Kanigher told her. "I didn't want to believe it was him."

"Yeah, he was damn stubborn about that. I couldn't keep him in with me while I planned the break. He smelled you in there. They all did."

Kanigher rubbed welling tears from his eyes. Sarge circled him and sat at his side, ready position, his head pitched toward Kanigher's, awaiting orders. The other dogs fell in around Kanigher, all but Sallygirl, who stayed with Haney.

"It's your squad, now, Cap," Haney said. "I guess, in a way, it always has been."

Kanigher raised an eyebrow. "What about the others?"

"This is everyone. It was me and Andru and the dogs."

Kanigher laid his hand atop Sarge's head. "All right, then. Let's move out."

He helped Haney onto her feet. Weak but steady, she pulled a couple of buzz tabs, one red and one blue, from one of Nightingale's pouches. She ate the red and fed Sallygirl the blue.

"A little boost to keep us vertical," she said.

Sallygirl stood with a whimper and walked out the door.

"Sallygirl's a smart one. No sense in wasting time," Haney said.

They moved out, Kanigher and Sarge right behind Sallygirl, the others behind them in a loose ring around Haney. Silence and night greeted them at the end of the alley. Bright Eyes, the other Shepherd, took point, and they moved through town using Kanigher's stop-and-go routine. They walked east through abandoned streets and dense shadows. Soon the buildings came farther apart, and treetops marked the open horizon outside town. A trash fire burned a block or two south of them, and the wind carried its heat and smoke across their path, filled with the odor of burning rubber and wood. The dogs hesitated as the cloud flooded their senses. Kanigher spied the fire glow on buildings in other parts of the city and wondered if the enemy knew about the dogs and had lit them on purpose. Regardless, they had another five klicks to reach their evac point. Kanigher sought an alternate route, but debris choked the nearest streets, leaving them only two options: double back or forge ahead. Kanigher urged the squad onward. They covered a few more yards, and then the dogs stiffened. Their ears pricked up. They scanned the night in every direction, enough warning for Kanigher to drop to a crouch, pulling Haney with him, shuffling them both behind the meager cover of a rubble pile.

The air whined, then the ground shook, and fire erased the night.

Broken rocks, concrete, and glass rained down on them.

When the echo of the explosion died, soldiers yelling replaced it.

He peered through a gap in the rubble. Ahead of their position sat a tank parked on a cross street, four soldiers around it, all gazing in the direction of his squad, weapons ready. One scrambled for a grenade launcher propped against the tank treads. Another buckled the strap under his helmet. Lit cigarettes glowed on the ground. If not for the soot and the heat from the trash fire, the dogs would've detected the cigarettes, the scents of tank oil, and human sweat. Kanigher chided himself for not turning back.

Haney rested her rifle in a crook in the rubble, then handed her sidearm to Kanigher, who took it even as his eyes scanned for the dogs. He saw only Sallygirl hunkered down behind a neighboring rubble mound, head on her paws, eyes glued to Haney.

The soldiers opened fire.

Shots chewed up the remnants of the street and pinged off the rubble. Haney returned fire, scattering the soldiers, all but the one holding the grenade launcher, who stood steady and aimed at their position, preparing to wipe them out with one shot—but he never fired.

Landing like a demon falling from the sky, Sarge hit him from the shadows, clenching his teeth on the soldier's neck even as he tore him sideways to the ground. The grenade launcher fell and rolled away. Bright Eyes and Marshmallow Soldier took down two other attackers, coming at them from out of their line of sight, hitting them hard and fast, bringing them to the ground, and lunging past the hands they raised in defense to rip at their necks and faces. Kanigher and Haney eased out from the rubble and fired on the fourth soldier, ripping bullets across his chest and dropping him. On the ground, the other soldiers all lay still, and the dogs withdrew from their corpses. A soldier in the tank snapped the hatch shut. The engine rumbled. The turret swiveled, bringing the gun around on Kanigher and Haney.

The sound of hoverbirds filled the air.

A flurry of barking rose from the dogs, then the animals scattered.

Sarge, Bug Eye, and Bright Eyes raced toward the tank and leapt onto its body.

Marshmallow Soldier and Nightingale bolted for Kanigher and Haney. Nightingale took Haney's wrist between her jaws and dragged her away. Marshmallow Soldier stood by Sallygirl, locked eyes with Kanigher, and barked three times. Kanigher took the hint. Careful not to drive the needles in her side any deeper, he slung Sallygirl across his shoulders in a firemen's carry. She whimpered in pain but settled against him. Behind him, a small explosion erupted. A shot from Sarge's mortar had broken the tank turret. Now the dogs worked the hatch with their energy weapons.

"Move out!" Kanigher shouted at them.

They couldn't hear him. He caught up to Haney.

"Use your link to order them to fall back and come with us," he said.

Haney nodded. Kanigher watched the dogs. Only Sarge lifted his head long enough to meet Kanigher's eyes. He wagged his tail, barked, and then resumed working at the hatch.

Kanigher started back, but Marshmallow Soldier grabbed his hand, urging him to continue. Lights from three hoverbirds painted the buildings now, closing on the tank's position. The dog's energy beams flared, and the hatch exploded free of its mounts.

Bug Eyes and Bright Eyes scrambled off the tank.

The hoverbirds dropped low, spotlights painting the vehicle. Like a living shadow, Sarge skipped the edge of the lights and vanished into the tank. Kanigher hesitated, waiting for the dog to reemerge, resisting Marshmallow dragging him onto a rubble-strewn back street that led away from town. A huge explosion rocked the night, spewing from the tank, catching the low-flying hoverbirds in its blast. Three more followed as the hoverships ignited.

Fire painted the sky.

Sarge's howls echoed in Kanigher's mind.

Haney faltered for a moment, knees weak, her expression blank, and Kanigher knew what she'd felt through her cyber-cowl, the last impressions from one of her dogs, one of his dogs.

They trudged to the evac point, keeping to shadows, the dogs picking a route over ground no tank could travel. Twice they heard enemy soldiers nearby, but Nightingale led them safely around them both times. Bug Eyes joined them one klick out. At the rendezvous, Bright Eyes sat waiting for them, a bloody gash in his side.

Kanigher didn't look for Sarge. Understanding gutted him and filled him with pride at the same time. After all those years, their reunion had lasted far too little time.

The squad held its position, hiding in the dark for an hour before their ride set down in the clearing. Kanigher hesitated, unwilling to leave his fallen dog behind, like so many others had been down through the history of soldier dogs. Then he thought of all that Sarge had given his comrades, all that Sarge had given him, and all he might do now with his freedom. He had no choice but to honor Sarge's sacrifice. Haney placed her hand on his shoulder. He let her lead him into the hoverbird. As it lifted into the dark, Kanigher's memories of Sarge howling blotted out the sound of its blades.

Killer Eye

These days all of Captain Ell Camden's dreams were silent. In them, people moved their mouths without speech, questions materialized stillborn on Camden's lips, and everything transpired in eerie tranquility. In one dream, Camden witnessed a jump plane crash. The graceful, silver craft plummeted into an open field where it erupted in a ball of fire and black smoke; but without the expected roar and shriek, the explosion seemed to blossom outward in slow motion. Often Camden dreamt of walking through a bright meadow where a whisperless wind swayed the chest-high grass all around him. Flowers speckled the landscape like a fluorescent snowfall. Roses grew everywhere, rising on long, thorny stems laden with heavy, blood-red flowers that bobbed and nodded as Camden passed, watching, straining toward him. He tried to call out, but the stillness devoured his cry. He awoke from just such a dream on the morning the kill orders came.

Snapping to consciousness, his body electrified with tension, Camden pawed the clutter on his nightstand until he unearthed a pack of stimarettes, then popped one between his lips and cracked its seal. Stimulating vapors cooled his throat and calmed his jittery nerves. He glanced at Lieutenant Ginny Nakata sleeping next to him, tangled in the bed sheets. Her black hair protruded in blunt spikes, and her torso rose and fell with her steady breathing. The ninth morning in three weeks he'd woken up beside her, and he knew the others—Major Davis Wyle, Captain Marnie Ambrov, and even Lieutenant Nakata herself—wondered if he were forming an over-attachment. Mission protocol allowed sex among members of the unit for physical and psychological release but not to foster romantic distractions. Camden expected a warning from Major Wyle, with orders to sleep alone for a while or go to bed with Captain Ambrov to restore the balance. He didn't care. He knew only that his dreams didn't unsettle him so much with Lieutenant Nakata beside him, an effect Captain Ambrov did not produce.

One of four soldiers assigned to Chang Station, all selected for their skills and psychological classification as "emotionally self-contained," natural loners, until recent weeks Camden had required only passing social contact to satisfy his human need for companionship. He and his unit were killers, weapons primed and waiting to be triggered. On duty for two years now—or more than a decade if you counted the nine-year journey from Earth to the Weed system—they faced two more years before completing their tour and shipping back to Earth, assuming an Earth remained to return to then.

Chang Station, one of thirty-five human outposts in the Weed system, formed a part of Operation Killer Eye. Each station housed four soldiers on the same twenty-two-year sniper stint. Most teams consisted of two men and two women, some of four soldiers of the same gender. All were assigned to monitor Arbor, the Weed homeworld, and run their outposts' armaments ranging from cluster bombs to nuclear missiles, grav phasers to particle-wave projectors. Chang Station, embedded in the rocky surface of Freeloader, a moon in orbit around the gas giant Vegas Strip, one of five planets in the system, sported a directed energy weapon. Other planets, their moons, and the asteroid belt that spiraled through the system harbored the other thirty-four KE stations.

With an hour to kill before reporting for duty, Camden slid from the bed and ambled into the adjoining observation chamber. The viewport offered a perfect vista of silver dust and craggy rocks. Pale amber and green light crested the horizon, heralding planet rise for Vegas Strip, named after the stormy, Technicolor cloud bands that lit it like infinite rows of neon lights. Camden finished his stimarette and tossed it into a flash incinerator. He reclined and waited until the emerald edge of Vegas Strip crept above the horizon like a cooling sun. Afterward, he headed for the shower unit, and a short time later, clean and alert, he dressed in uniform and gently roused Lieutenant Nakata. She smiled and slipped from the sheets to pull on the sweatpants and T-shirt she'd left crumpled on the floor, then padded away.

The room felt emptier without her, a sensation Camden hadn't noticed before the past few weeks. He'd never minded being alone before, and in fact, had often preferred it. The change heralded a potential problem for a soldier with two years left in his solitary tour of duty. From the top drawer of his nightstand, he took the photo plate he'd brought in his small allowance of personal items and activated the slideshow, a handful of pictures of his parents and his brother, Varrow. He and Varrow tried to stick together after a plane crash orphaned them, but bureaucratic artifice forced them apart. Over the years, they'd kept in touch and helped each other, when possible, until they'd both enlisted, and the military separated them for good. Ell hadn't heard from his brother for more than a decade when news came six weeks ago, already thirteen months old, that during a ship-to-ship skirmish, the Weeds had captured Varrow with a hundred others, all now presumed dead.

Ell imagined his brother fighting and falling, dragged off and trapped like a lab rat in an utterly silent starcraft piloted by alien beings. The Weeds had earned their name for their appearance: lanky stalk-like bodies and multiple, asymmetrical limbs that resembled branches and leaves, topped by a bulbous head like a cross between a rose blossom and a human brain. Their ships were said to be deathly quiet because the Weeds communicated telepathically—reason one for the war, because Weed telepathy didn't extend to humans, so they failed to recognize people as sentient beings, classifying them instead as pests for extermination from civilized places. That theory proved the most popular anyway, cooked up by experts after decades of study, although no one knew for sure.

Weed telepathy, though, gave humanity its only edge in the conflict. It worked across vast, even interstellar distances, so the Weeds had never developed any form of audible or electronic communication. They traveled in silent ships, lived in silent cities, and sent no signals through space. Thus, they were unable to intercept or interpret human communication via radio, laser, or subspace wave, a weakness that allowed humans to infiltrate the Weed system and keep contact without exposing themselves. Thus, Camden had come to live in a cramped and Spartan base on an airless moon, where his sole task concerned the maintenance of a directed energy weapon, dubbed "the torch," awaiting orders to fire.

He clicked off the photo plate and put it away.

Heading for the command deck, Camden felt grateful for the dull tapping of his footsteps, for the tinny clang when he knocked on the bulkhead, for the presence of all the small sounds that filled Chang Station. The alert siren sounded as he descended the ladder between levels, and his heart leapt at the raw, dizzying wail that filled the cramped corridors. He dropped the last few feet of the tube and darted along a short passage to the command deck, where he met Major Wyle, his face taut with anxiety.

"Pre-signal, code Foxtrot-Kilo-3-1-Niner," he announced, then looking up, "Morning, Captain Camden."

"Major Wyle," Camden said as he took his post and launched the mandatory diagnostic check of their decrypting array. "System check," he said, then when a green light flashed, added, "All channels open and clear."

"Pray for good news," Wyle said.

In anywhere from fifteen minutes to two hours, a message, already as much as a year old, would follow the pre-signal, traveling from the Killer Eye command ship four luminal months out from the Weed system. Command communications were infrequent; the last had provided the required notification to Camden, as next of kin, of his brother's assumed death. Captain Ambrov entered, took the gunner's station, and initiated the priming sequence to prep the torch.

"What's the word? We going live?"

"Don't know yet," Wyle said.

A moment later, Lieutenant Nakata arrived, fulfilling the regulations requirement that all stations be attended during communications transmissions.

"Captain Camden, your turn to call odds," she said.

"Right," Camden said. "Okay, given we're still technically under ceasefire, I'd say 500,000 to 1 we're getting kill orders. 50 to 1 it's a war report, 20 to 1 it's just a morale booster."

"What about peace?" Ambrov asked. "The last war report sounded promising for further negotiations."

Wyle scoffed. "Nothing but spin. How far do you think they can get with the Weeds by trading holographic projections of mathematical equations?"

"Gotta start somewhere," Ambrov said.

"All right," Camden said. "Odds on peace are a million to 1. Get your bets on the table."

"Wait," Nakata said. "What about a false signal? The last war report also warned the Weeds might be catching onto our communications tech. Maybe it's a trick."

"Rumors, that's all, to keep us on our guard," Wyle said.

"Rumors from almost two years ago," Nakata said. "Could be the Weeds learn fast. Captain Camden?"

"Fine, 100,000 to 1 it's a ruse," Camden offered.

"Better odds than peace or a kill order," Nakata said.

"You're making me paranoid. Now, open channels with our sister stations for verification," Camden said. "Let's find out if anyone else is activated."

Each soldier scribbled an amount on a scrap of paper and tossed it into a small depression on the central command table. They'd started the no-limit betting game and kept a running tally in honor of Vegas Strip, and they bet on anything they could. Captain Ambrov was up $653,486 over everyone else, and she insisted she aimed to collect every cent when they were all discharged.

After placing her bet, Lieutenant Nakata arranged the controls to relay between the four nearest stations. The machinery surrounding them produced a steady hum, and tinny beeps came from Captain Ambrov's monitor as she powered the torch. The directed energy weapon could strike a target as small as a single Weed or as sprawling as a city. The Killer Eye program gave humanity a chance to hurt the Weeds badly enough to end the conflict. Fighting head-to-head, the Weeds seemed unbeatable. They'd become a spacefaring race hundreds of years before humankind, with faster ships, better weapons, and communications at the speed of thought, which enabled thousands of them to act as one when executing battle tactics. Remaining unpredictable and attacking by surprise gave humanity its only chance. Still, the Weeds had forced the Navy almost all the way back to Earth before the latest ceasefire. The next time hostilities reached a fever pitch, the Killer Eyes would certainly go hot.

Lately, it seemed more and more imminent. Observations of the Arbor indicated construction of a new starship type that would dwarf their others, one possibly intended for a final assault against Earth. Expert analysis estimated a decade before it could make an attack. Most of the human population held out hope for a peace agreement before then, but two previous ceasefires had failed, and the current one seemed destined for stalemate as long as the Weeds rejected the concept of humans as beings equal to themselves in sentience and dignity.

Camden wondered if his brother were truly dead. No one taken prisoner by the Weeds had ever returned, so military policy declared those captured as killed in action after thirty days. Maybe Varrow still lived, caged in some silent prison where the Weeds studied him. Or maybe they'd dissected him alive. Or incinerated him. Hundreds of tales about what the Weeds did to prisoners made the rounds without a shred of evidence to prove any of them.

The uncertainty made the loss all the more painful. A military death declaration worked to close the files, but for Camden, it only emphasized how alone he was now with his entire family ushered into oblivion. He had only the military left, a military that had made him more machine than a man, a component in a sophisticated gun. His physical needs were rigidly satiated, his emotional needs neatly cataloged and accounted for, and he and all the KE operatives were told they were special, that as Killer Eyes, they were granted responsibilities and privileges beyond those of common soldiers. The freedom, the self-reliance, the isolation only disguised the fact that KE soldiers were no more than carefully chosen, strictly trained trigger pieces—extensions of the military intelligence machine. With minor variations, the soldiers on all thirty-five Killer Eye stations were the same, as if stamped from clay on a factory line. They ate, they slept, they excreted, they copulated, but mostly they did their assigned duties and spent as much time alone as possible. Like members of a cult. For the first time in his tour of duty, that reality bothered Camden. He hadn't considered it before Varrow died, before the dreams started, before the scent of Lieutenant Nakata's sweat lingered in his memory for days after sharing her bed. Now the irony proved inescapable—to fight the Weeds, they'd shed their humanity and become in many ways exactly like their enemy.

Camden's gaze drifted to Lieutenant Nakata. He wondered if she felt any of this, if she'd found herself drawn to him like he'd been to her, or if she were just going along with him out of duty.

"Comm channel check. Confirm status," Lieutenant Nakata said, snapping Camden out of his thoughts.

He ran the program and scowled. "No contact with our sister stations."

"How can that be?" Nakata asked. "Interference?"

"Between us and all four of our sister bases simultaneously? Unlikely," Camden said. "All readings are clear. We've had minimal sunspot activity for three weeks."

"Maybe technical failure?" she said. "Our comm gear is due for maintenance in two days."

"Checking now," Camden said. "All equipment appears fine. Could be failure on *one* of the other bases but not *all five* simultaneously. Do we have line of sight with any of the stations?"

Lieutenant Nakata summoned a fresh display on her monitor. "Philip Station will be in position in forty-five seconds. Go to Morse laser for contact confirmation?"

Monitoring the conversation, Major Wyle glanced at Lieutenant Nakata's screen and said, "We've never used the signal laser, Lieutenant Nakata. It's a last resort. The Weeds could see it. How long will we have line of sight with Philip Station?"

"Approximately nineteen minutes before planet rise puts Vegas Strip between us and them," Nakata told him.

"Let's wait and see if our orders come through," Wyle said.

"Major Wyle, all D-E-W systems active," Ambrov said. "Targeting systems operational. The torch is primed and ready to light."

"Thank you, captain."

The alert siren blared back to life with dizzying urgency. Major Wyle darted to his station while Camden and Captain Nakata managed the incoming signal.

"That was fast," Nakata said.

"Record time," Ambrov said. "Anyone else getting a bad feeling about this?"

"Quiet," Wyle said.

Camden's fingers clacked over his keyboard, assigning computers to decrypt their orders. A cold draft of tension crept through the room. The signal transmitted for several minutes then ended. Major Wyle's eyes remained glued to his monitor as the decrypted orders scrolled across his screen. He read them twice and cross-checked them against his mission journal.

"Is that it?" he said.

"Yes, sir," Camden said. "It cut short."

Major Wyle turned to Lieutenant Nakata. "Status of comm channels, lieutenant?"

"Still off-line, sir."

"Line of sight with Philip Station?"

"Open for another nine minutes."

"All right, activate the laser. We need confirmation," Wyle said.

"Sir?" Nakata asked.

"We have been assigned a target and ordered to fire," Wyle told them. "I want confirmation."

"What is our target, sir?" Ambrov asked.

Major Wyle tapped his keyboard and relayed the decrypted portion of their orders to the other stations. On each monitor appeared: "Arbor Spaceport Omega, 09:00," a prime target in the planet's southern hemisphere.

"That's it?" Ambrov asked.

"It came in segmented and heavily coded." Camden's fingers crawled over his console. "More was embedded in the transmission, but the signal ended before we received the final close code, so we can't decrypt the rest."

"Our orders are incomplete," Wyle said.

"Incomplete but clear, major," Nakata said.

"We could be missing something important, like a secondary target or a firing condition," Wyle said. "I won't proceed on half-baked information."

"The rest was probably a war report, an update on negotiations," Camden said.

"Or lack of them," Ambrov added.

"Commencing signal to Philip Station," Nakata announced.

The four soldiers waited, outwardly still, yet each of them running mental drills as their battle training swept them into fight mode. They imagined the strike, the inevitable Weed retaliation, and wondered what had happened to bring about activation of the Killer Eyes. If one base acted alone, the Weeds would almost certainly locate and destroy it and eventually all the others. Only if all of the KE stations fired simultaneously to devastate Arbor world could any of them hope to survive. There always existed the possibility that command needed one heavy attack to make a point to the Weeds, win an advantage in negotiations, or eliminate a critical target. That made any single KE station or all of them expendable.

"No reply from Philip Station," Nakata said. "Their sensors should've sighted our laser by now."

Wyle stood and rubbed his forehead with his thumb and forefinger. "Captain Camden, care to give odds on whether or not Philip Station still exists?"

"No, sir," Camden said. "Bets are already on the table."

"Consider this a new hand," Wyle said. "We all know what happens after we light the torch. Unless it's a prelude to an all-out attack against Arbor, the Weeds will find and destroy us. For all we know, that's what happened to Philip Station after they acted on earlier orders. Or maybe something went wrong over there, and Philip Station is down by a quirk of fate. They could've been gone for weeks. Our last communication with them was—what?"

"Seven months ago," Nakata said.

"The loss of radio communication with the other stations suggests something more at work," Wyle said.

"Like maybe the Weeds are jamming our transmissions," Camden said. "The kill order could be a trick to flush us out. The truncated signal would camouflage the fact that the Weeds don't have the close codes needed to authenticate the orders. They're hoping we'll overlook that and give ourselves away."

"So, they're fishing," Wyle said. "They've got an idea we're here, but they don't know for sure. It's possible."

"That would explain the silence from our sister stations," Nakata said. "Maybe they figured this out ahead of us and went dark."

"So, of course, we go blundering in with the damn Morse laser," Ambrov said.

"Unlikely the Weeds'll notice our laser with Vegas Strip so close by," Wyle said. "Anyway, we've got bigger problems to worry about."

"Such as?" Nakata asked.

"Do we fire?" Wyle said.

"We have orders," Ambrov said.

"Incomplete, unverified orders," Wyle said. "The absence of a close code aborts authorization. For all we know, this could be a drill or a targeting test—something that would've been disclosed in the portion we lost."

"Or KE command could've been destroyed before completing transmission," said Camden. "When have we ever gotten orders so fast after a pre-signal? They were rushing for a reason."

"You think the ceasefire broke?" Nakata asked.

Camden shrugged.

"How long would it take to replace KE command?" Ambrov said.

"Eighteen months at least before another ship can be moved into position," Wyle said. "If that's the case, then we're now under the direct command of General Cuidera."

"Which leaves us with a three-year turnaround if we request confirmation." Camden grimaced. "Our orders are to fire in just under two hours."

"Reassess the transmission, Captain Camden. Maybe we missed something," Wyle said.

"I've checked it six times, sir. We've gotten everything we're going to out of it."

Major Wyle settled into his seat and peered at his monitor while he replayed the transmission, watching the progress bar track across the width of his screen only to halt and freeze just before the end, leaving him with nothing more than a jarringly succinct time and target.

"All right," he said, turning back to the others. "We're cut off, and it's up to us to decide. Anyone have a problem with that?"

"We have our orders right here." Camden tapped his screen. "What's there to decide? At 09:00, we fire."

"You're not worried it might be a Weed trick?"

"Does it matter? We take out one of their key spaceports," Camden said.

"And give ourselves away," Wyle said. "Maybe blow cover for the whole KE program."

"It won't matter if all stations fire."

"We don't know that will happen," Wyle said.

"If the orders are legit, then all stations probably received a target. Maybe some of them even received the full transmission. If it's a trick, if the Weeds are out there fishing, if they've gotten their hands on radio tech, and they're jamming our communications and transmitting blind, that means everyone's getting the same orders. They'll fire."

"Not without verification," Wyle said. "Absence of verification negates an order. Effectively we have no kill order. That's protocol. We're out here on our own, connected by the slenderest of threads to the rest of the military. We are not a bunch of cowboys. Procedure is the only thing that has held us together since day one, and that's how it has to be now. Captain Ambrov, power down the D-E-W."

"Wait," Camden said. "Have you forgotten what we all enlisted to do? We're here to defend Earth."

"We won't do that by launching an unauthorized attack that could jeopardize our entire mission," Wyle said.

"What if they're counting on us?" Camden asked. "Waiting for us to soften up the Weeds before bringing the fleet into position?"

"We'd have received a war report and orders," Wyle said.

"We just did," Camden said.

"No, what we've got is an unverified signal from an unidentified source. Less than an hour ago, you—yourself—called better odds on it being a deception than a kill order," Wyle said.

"Yeah, and Captain Ambrov really thinks she's going to collect her winnings from us after our tour ends," Camden said. "You can't take that seriously."

"What I take seriously is not gambling with our mission," Wyle said. "Captain Camden, report to your quarters until further notice. I will not have you brewing dissent."

Camden stiffened as though he'd been struck. He clamped his mouth shut, saluted stiffly, and then exited the command room with a glance at Lieutenant Nakata. Her worried expression burned like a bonfire in contrast to the pale passiveness on Captain Ambrov's face, and though he wasn't sure why, Camden took comfort from it. Then he entered the well and climbed to the upper level.

He bypassed his room in favor of the observation chamber. Vegas Strip filled the sky with saccharine ribbons of color, the sight of which Camden never wearied. He knew if he ever returned to Earth, this of all the things he'd done and seen since his enlistment would remain brightest in his memory. The mesmerizing whorls of color swirling in bands that seemed to spin like the cutting edge of a power saw. The light and dark flashes of storm activity. The contradictory sensation of serenity that such wonderful chaos fostered in him. This proof of the sheer wonder of the universe. This reminder of the magnitude of humanity's accomplishments in challenging cold, harsh space and conquering it. He wondered if the Weeds saw Vegas Strip the way he did, if any single living creature among them could look upon the planet and experience the awe it inspired in him.

On a whim, he went to the door control panel. He punched in his access code, called up the past six months' entry records, and scrolled through the list. His own code appeared over and over again, sometimes two or three times a day, and here and there, he saw Lieutenant Nakata's, and less frequently but still regularly Captain Ambrov's. Major Wyle's appeared only once, logged in eight weeks ago barely a minute after Lieutenant Nakata's, suggesting a mood-setting rendezvous, something done out of facility rather than desire. Camden wondered why Major Wyle rarely came here, if the sight held no majesty or fascination for him, or if he truly preferred passing time sequestered in his quarters. None of the KE soldiers socialized much, but a thing as raw and powerful as Vegas Strip possessed a gravity that tugged at primal human nature, something, perhaps, Major Wyle had lost or forgotten or, worse, feared, something he might prefer not to rediscover.

Camden spared a last glance at Vegas Strip's stunning luminosity. Then he left the observation chamber for the armory, where he selected a shotgun and a pulse rifle to complement his uniform sidearm and prayed he wouldn't need any of them. He steeled himself and returned to the command deck.

It surprised Camden how calmly he stepped through the entryway and leveled the shotgun in Major Wyle's direction. No one spoke for several seconds. In that time, the color leached from the major's face, and his bearing turned quite brittle. Captain Ambrov rested her hand on her sidearm. Captain Nakata gasped at Camden with pure shock.

"Ell," she said.

The way his name rose from her lips, the way she breathed it as though it were part of the elements that sustained her life sent shivers down Camden's spine, and in that moment, any flagging doubt remaining within him evaporated.

"Captain Ambrov," Camden said. "Power up the D-E-W and prepare targeting coordinates for Spaceport Omega at 09:00."

"I'm sorry, captain, but no, I already have my orders," she said.

"Yes, you do, and Major Wyle won't object now if you follow them. He's gotten a little confused today, but we're going to help him through it," Camden said.

"This is mutiny," Ambrov said. "Put the weapons down before someone gets hurt."

"Sorry, Marnie," Camden said, watching Ambrov's face crinkle at the sound of her first name. "Mutiny is when you don't follow orders. Now you can do as I told you, or I will fire on Major Wyle."

Moving with fluid speed, Ambrov drew her sidearm and aimed it at Camden. "Then I'll have to kill you where you stand."

Camden hadn't expected such a swift reaction, hadn't anticipated her taking Wyle's side. They made a running joke of her hatred of the Weeds, and he'd assumed she'd leap at a chance to hurt them, but she possessed strong discipline. Camden considered the possibility he'd made a fatal mistake. He didn't want to kill Major Wyle, wasn't sure he could act against Marnie before she killed him, didn't want to hurt or kill her, but they had their orders, and something deep inside Camden urged him forward, insisted that at 09:00 hours their weapon must fire.

"I'm sorry, Marnie, but I intend to see that weapon fired as ordered. If you need to see Major Wyle and me dead to prevent that, that's your choice," Camden said.

"Two people can man this station as well as four." Captain Ambrov cocked her weapon.

"No!" Lieutenant Nakata's voice shattered the icy tension. In a second, the balance shifted. With Lieutenant Nakata's sidearm prodding her torso, Captain Ambrov lowered her gun.

"Ginny." Her name trembled on Camden's lips.

"I trust you, Ell," Nakata said. "I really do. It's like those dreams you told me about. Maybe you know something the rest of us don't. I don't know, but I know *you*, trust *you*."

Ginny prodded Captain Ambrov with her gun barrel. "Now, power up the D-E-W, *Marnie*."

Captain Ambrov grimaced and complied. Camden inched across the room, gently removed Major Wyle's sidearm, then tucked it into a pocket of his uniform. The major did not resist.

"Have a seat, major," Camden said. "This will all be over soon."

"What if you're wrong?" the major asked.

"If the orders are legit, we're doing what we're supposed to. If the Weeds caught on to our communications tech, then we've lost the last hope we have of keeping one step ahead of them in this bloody war. If they track us, screw with our communications, we've lost the only advantage that's been keeping us alive. Either way, we need to hit them hard with everything we've got right now—before they get their act together."

"What do you mean?"

"If the signal is a Weed ruse, it's a clumsy one. A kill order broadcast blindly? And jamming the signal? Maybe they've got an idea how the tech works, but they don't understand enough yet to fully use it against us. Like little kids picking up a comm set for the first time. They get the idea. They might try to talk into the earpiece because that's where the voice comes from, but they'll learn. They'll get better. They'll steal our only edge in this fight. No matter where the signal came from, it's now or never."

Captain Ambrov backed away from the control deck and sat beside Major Wyle. "D-E-W is primed, firing coordinates programmed."

Ginny confirmed the gun settings. Camden tried to clear his mind, tried to think of what position Vegas Strip would hold now, tried to summon the vision of Ginny in his bed that morning and how her hair and skin smelled. He tried to recall his brother's voice and the rough way he shook hands. Then he dove back deep into memories of his parents, whom he'd known for precious few years. He wondered what they would've made of his life and Varrow's, whether they would've been proud or horrified, whether or not their presence would've made things turn out differently. The time passed too quickly, not at all like Camden expected, and when the moment came, he strode to the gunner's station and eased Ginny aside. He chose this—his decision, his act—lashing out at the inhuman enemy, at the inhumanity required to fight them, inhumanity that jeopardized humanity's survival as much as it protected it. If there were one like him on every KE station, then perhaps they really had a chance. The digital countdown ended. He entered the execution order and then—*listened.*

Unseen machinery whirred and vibrated. The entire station quivered with a deep, basso thrumming that ran through the soldiers' bodies and set their teeth chattering. The entire place throbbed like a beating heart, its pulse building on the rising whine of energy pooling in the chamber. Camden listened to the others breathing: Major Wyle sucking in air in curt, staccato inhalations; Captain Ambrov huffing with frustration; Ginny panting with shallow gasps. Camden realized he held his breath, then exhaled in a long stream and let his chest rise and fall once more. The external hissing of the torch firing lasted several minutes, then ended.

Camden imagined the searing blast of ivory fire pouring out of the dark structure of steel and titanium embedded in Freeloader's harsh granite, pictured it slicing through space, progressing minute by minute, second by second until it reached its target with merciless and incinerating fury. The blast would strike ground at 09:12. When the time came, the order fulfilled, Camden dropped his weapons, slumped in the gunner's chair, and sighed. Minutes passed in corrosive quiet. No one moved; no one spoke.

"Did…" Ginny finally said, "Did the other stations fire?"

Captain Ambrov swiveled to the nearest keyboard and summoned up the sensor outputs. "Everything's flat," she said. "No, wait! I've got an incoming signal."

The radio comm crackled. Captain Ambrov shunted the transmission to speakers.

"Philip Station to Chang Station," a voice said. "Come in, Chang Station."

Tendrils of ice crept through Camden's mind.

"Come in Chang Station."

"This is Chang Station," Ambrov said. "We read you, Philip Station. What is your status?"

"Chang Station, our status is active. We are at war and have fired upon the target," the voice said. "We have confirmation from Addams Station, Lodi Station, and Tesla Station. Please confirm weapon discharge."

"Discharge confirmed," Ambrov breathed into the mouthpiece. "Philip Station, our order signal was cut short. Can you confirm orders?"

"Negative," came back Philip Station. "Orders were false. Repeat. Orders were a false signal from the Weeds, combined with a jamming transmission. We have destroyed the source, but the situation left us no choice but to act. Check your radar, Chang Station, because we are not done fighting yet."

Ginny moved to a workstation and ordered up the radar display.

"Ships," she said.

"Hundreds," Ambrov said. "Some of them huge."

"Looks like the Weeds finished their new destroyer ahead of schedule," Camden said. "Marnie, can you get a bead on one of the big ones with the torch?"

Grappling with shock, Ambrov nodded and dashed around to the gunner's seat.

"You were right, Ell." Ginny reached for the scraps of folded paper in the center console. Camden placed his hand on hers and stopped her.

"It doesn't matter," he said. "Gambling only counts when you've got something to lose."

Marnie ignited the torch again. Silent and stone-faced, Major Wyle resumed his station without a glance at the others. Chang Station sang with energy and the strain of cold metal shifting and churning together. The hum of the blast filled everyone's ears. Camden turned to a keyboard, plotting their next target. In his mind appeared the image of the energy beam lancing through space, cutting darkness, destined to claim the lives of hundreds, even thousands of Weeds—and silent all the while. Silent in its glory; silent in its devastation. As silent as Camden's dreams and the forever stilled voices of his parents and his brother. He lifted his head, desperate in that moment for the sound of something human, something meaningful, and said: "Ginny."

Politicos

The applause of nearly a million people shook the New Omaha Civic Arena as they cheered the luminous effigy that straddled the central stage. Four projections of the figure's bust hovered at the compass points high overhead, and shimmering balloons dropped from the ceiling drizzled through the faces. Brassy music blared as machines spat out multicolored snow that melted as it landed on the roaring crowd. Kogi Anderson cheered with them from the wings, caught in a fervor rising from a deep sense of satisfaction in a risky career move and eight years of hard work finally paying off.

Onstage, Governor Sam Durjaya stood shining in the light of his flickering projection, arms raised in a victorious pose. His mammoth double mimicked him then he clicked a remote control that froze it in position. Anderson admired how the projectors smoothed over the imperfections of the governor's seventy-three years, darkening the gray waves of his hair and lending him a look of wizened vigor. When the last of the cameras surrounding him switched off, Durjaya rubbed his jaw with spidery fingers. His bright eyes fought signs of fatigue. Anderson recognized their excited light from the governor's past appearances and from studying decades-old videos of Durjaya's early stump speeches, when his audiences had numbered in the hundreds at best. Tonight, tens of millions of people watched from home, and hundreds of millions more would catch pieces of the governor's speech in news streams around the world. This time belonged to Durjaya. Anderson took pride in serving as chief of staff for such a consummate survivor, one of the few old-school politicos to chart a successful course through the Reconstitution, bridging the reviled past and the modern era it had birthed. When so many of his contemporaries had jumped ship into the private sector, retired, or died, Sam Durjaya never gave up hope or lost his touch for gaining the people's trust.

Anderson met the governor as he withdrew behind the towering, velvet stage curtains. Durjaya wasted no time tugging open the zipper of his cumbersome Reston-McGarvey jumpsuit. Long ago fodder for memes and movie gags, its badges and logos declaring his campaign contributors, official endorsements, and political allegiances made the governor look like an old-fashioned NASCAR driver, except it sparkled like a mirrorball from the metallic threads woven into the patches and neon spangles tagged with anti-counterfeiting RFID chips. Anderson knew Durjaya missed the dark suits, silk ties, and polished shoes that comprised the old-school politicos' uniform. He sympathized. Forty years the governor's junior, Anderson had come to appreciate the old style, but these days the Reston-McGarvey Act dictated how public officials dressed and how they lived, and that meant full transparency, 24/7.

A chipset and fiber-optic camera implanted beneath Durjaya's left ear recorded his entire life, sending data via a secure ether-cloud link to a remote system, where it became evidence-in-waiting should the slightest whiff of impropriety ever arise. Every politician accepted a so-called honesty rig upon declaring their first candidacy for everything from town clerk to senator, and every politician received a weekly online rating of their public speeches, ranked for consistency across their entire career, allowing the public to judge them at a glance. Anderson helped Durjaya navigate the modern political system, keeping him in compliance and his public ranking high.

He grabbed Durjaya's jumpsuit before it crumpled to the stage and handed it off to a waiting assistant, then he led the governor into the recesses of the sprawling arena. Durjaya's speech had riled the behind-the-scenes crowd as much as the audience, and a backstage throng of technicians, managers, clerks, and even opposition staffers waited to greet the man. Anderson signaled the security detail to stay alert as the governor waded among the pressing bodies. Durjaya greeted each awestruck grin with a warm nod, shook every extended hand twice, and absorbed their congratulations with humility until Anderson ushered him into his dressing rooms.

As his chief-of-staff closed the door, shutting out the crowd, Durjaya stopped in the center of the small lounge of the suite assigned him for the duration of the convention. Soundproofed walls blocked the din outside, but the floor still quivered with stamping feet.

"Feel that, Andy?" Durjaya loosened his tie and top button. "If I were a less cautious man, I'd say I just clinched the nomination."

"They love you, governor," Anderson said. "For-real love, not just hero worship. You spun magic out there tonight."

The governor walked to a small bar and poured himself a scotch. Ice tinkled as he swished it around the glass. "Well, thank you, Andy. So glad you approve. Couldn't have done it without you, son."

"If you don't mind me saying so, governor, the time for caution is long gone."

Anderson sat at a desk in the corner. His fingers clacked over a keyboard, and a dark, razor-thin monitor screen brightened, painting his boyish face with a cold glow. "The polls give you a twenty-three percent lead over Morlant, seventeen percent over Kendall, and you're ahead of all the others by thirty percent or more. If the general election were held today, you'd easily beat any member of any other party by at least nine percent—oh, wait—*make that twelve percent.* Apparently, part of the crowd rushed the stage when the tech crew tried to clear your display for the next speaker. They're demanding your speech be replayed in full. I wouldn't be surprised if your opponents concede tonight."

Durjaya's knees popped as he settled into the plush armchair beside the comms deck. "Andy, my friend, let's not get ahead of ourselves, count our chickens and all that, but I will admit this is an extremely positive sensation." The governor lifted the tumbler to his face and savored the aroma of twenty-one-year-old scotch. "I came close to this almost twenty-five years ago. Then Atlanta happened, and the whole damn house of cards collapsed. Scary, scary time. Thornton's screw-up put all our necks on the block. When Reston-McGarvey passed, I thought,

'I'm going to lose everything I've worked so hard for.' But I didn't... I didn't. If that bad bit of business about Robinson and that Illinois sex cult hadn't disqualified him in the next election, though, my career might've ended right there."

"Michigan forgave you. Now the rest of the country is tripping over itself to support you."

"Andy," Durjaya said. "Pour yourself a drink, son. You've earned it."

"Thank you, sir."

Anderson moved to the bar and filled a glass with ice and scotch. He grabbed the remote lying there, activated the paper-thin television screen pasted onto the wall, and lowered the sound to a murmur. Pundits and analysts picked over the meat of Governor Durjaya's speech, but even the shrillest of naysayers found little to criticize. It was as if no other man in history had ever felt the pulse of the nation as clearly and powerfully as Durjaya did. The governor's natural political charm combined with Anderson's tech-media savvy made for a great combination. Unbeatable. Anderson could've stayed with his old party, Order Established, for twenty years and never reached this far, obtained this much power.

"Maybe it truly was all for the best," the governor said. "The outrage, backlash, and cynicism. The uncertainty that followed Atlanta. It sure as hell gave folks the juice to root out the corruption. Took a lot of good men and women down, too, though. Ruined a lot of lives. But that's how we played the big game back then. Things only happened when we fed all the hungry mouths of the powerful and all the kingmakers received their offerings. Nobody could stay clean in that environment. *Nobody.* Not a perfect system, but it got the job done most of the time. It was good enough for my great-grandparents when they came here from Bhopal, for my grandparents, for my parents after them. Now people expect us to keep our promises to the letter, adhere to our principles dogmatically, and they toss us out on our asses when they don't like the results. You *gotta* love it."

Durjaya paused, sipped his drink, and closed his eyes. The governor rarely spoke about the old days, especially with such candor, but on an emotionally charged night like this one, it seemed he couldn't contain it.

"To be honest, Andy," he said, "the whole damn turn of events, Reconstitution, the new laws, the changes in public opinion, it's all been a relief when you come right down to it. Can't remember the last time I had to wait on the results of a focus group before stating my position. Or when I last looked the other way on a bad policy to avoid upsetting some loudmouth part of my constituency in an election year. Do you remember the Visitor Voter Act? No, before your time, wasn't it? Damn harebrained scheme to sell democracy-tourism packages and stuff the ballots with votes from anyone with enough money to pay the going fare. We were hot to give the whole damn country away just to stay in office, hold onto power. Well, good riddance to all that. It feels good to say 'No' when I want to and 'Yes' when I mean it, and get out there and lead the folks. So, go on, Andy. Hold your finger high and tell me which way the wind blows."

Anderson resumed surfing the net, trawling the news, assessing reports and reactions from all quarters. "I'd say this is a great moment in history, governor. People will look back at this and say, 'That was a turning point.'"

"Feels that way, doesn't it?" Durjaya said. "Justifies all that hoopla and scandal back when I wooed you away from Order Established. Proves my personal philosophy that it's more important to win over one man fully than a dozen half-heartedly because that one man will go out and convince others by virtue of his conviction. In that regard, Andy, you've worked miracles."

"I've only been doing my job."

An electronic chime rang, and a light beside the door lit.

"I'm sorry, governor. I left instructions that you weren't to be disturbed for at least half an hour," Anderson said.

"Don't sweat it. Just go see who it is."

Anderson cracked the door open, blocking the governor's view of the hallway outside. "Yes? What is it?"

A bronze glow filled the opening, and a low voice asked, "I want to see Governor Sam Durjaya."

"He can't be disturbed right now. You'll have to make an appointment—*what the hell!?*" Anderson backed into the room, stumbling.

A slender, young man followed him, clutching a coal-black weapon of cast resin in one hand. With his other hand, he reached back and shut the door. He wore a plain, three-piece suit and resembled any average staffer scurrying around backstage that night.

"Please sit, Mr. Anderson. Governor, stay where you are." Without lowering his gun, the man crossed the room in three strides and smashed the comms deck against the floor. "Let's keep this amongst the three of us for the moment, if you don't mind."

"Who are you? How did you get in here?" Anderson said.

"If you've harmed my security officers, you'll pay. Count on it," Durjaya said.

"Your guards are fine. They're right outside the door, and if you cooperate, I'll be gone before they ever know I've been here. I don't want to hurt them. I don't want to hurt anyone. I'm here to deliver a message." The man stared at Durjaya, his weapon matching his gaze. "Governor, it's time for you to drop out of this race."

"Are you insane?" Anderson said.

Durjaya took a deep breath, sipped his drink, and then set the glass down on a table. "Coming from behind a gun, that sounds more like an ultimatum than a message. What's your name, son?"

"I'm no one you know."

"That's not what I asked. I don't answer to threats. You want to talk to me? Tell me your name."

Durjaya stood, closed the top button of his shirt, and tightened his tie.

The stranger hesitated, then said, "All right, it's Sorenson."

"Mr. Sorenson, then," Durjaya said. "You asked us to relax. I'd relax a whole lot more if you'd put that gun down. I'm always willing to talk. Anyone who knows me knows that. Violence never solves anything among reasonable men."

"I'm sorry, but I believe you'll hear me better with a gun in my hand," Sorenson said. "That is, unless you're ready to concede."

"By dropping my bid for the nomination?"

"Yes. Call in your publicist to make the announcement. You can be on the air inside of fifteen minutes."

"If I don't?"

"You'll soon be a very unhappy man. You, too, Mr. Anderson." Sorenson spoke without hesitation as if his prediction had already come true.

"I'm a hair's breadth from winning. Why the hell would I drop out now?"

"A lot of reasons, but the most important to you is that if you continue your bid for the presidency, my associates will release information to the press that we're certain you'd prefer to see withheld. Information that will ruin not only your political career but quite possibly your ability to conduct yourself in American society," Sorenson told him.

Durjaya laughed. "Mr. Sorenson, you haven't got a thing on me. All the skeletons in my closet got dragged into the light twenty-five years ago during Reconstitution, and I haven't restocked since then. You're a couple of decades too late to blackmail me."

"This information isn't about something you've done, governor. It's about something you'll do during your first term as president," Sorenson said.

"You have some kind of crystal ball showing you the future? Anderson's right. You're insane," Durjaya said.

"I hoped you might put the pieces together on your own. You know how I know," Sorenson said. "Anyway, you'll get the nomination. You'll win the White House by a historic, overwhelming majority. You'll skate through reelection and serve two terms. There will be a grass-roots movement to allow you a third, a fourth, and beyond, but it will fail. You'll retire a beloved national icon, hailed as the man who launched a golden age of peace and prosperity. Five years later, you'll die. If those things happen, you'll also set in motion events that result in the deaths of more than two-thirds of the world's population fifteen years after you leave office. I can't tell you the specifics. Even with foreknowledge, there's no way you can alter the outcome of your presidency other than to never take office."

"Is this a fucking joke?" Anderson said. "Did Morlant send you here? Are you from Order Established?"

Sorenson shook his head. "I've been sent by people who haven't been born yet. To them, this is history."

"You realize how this sounds," Durjaya said.

"Of course," Sorenson said. "To most people, at least, but not anyone familiar with the research of Ford Martin."

"Who the hell is Ford Martin?" Anderson said.

"Martin's laboratory is in Detroit. Governor Durjaya has been working with him for decades. Correct, governor? Ever since Reconstitution, when you assumed the role of liaison between him and the White House. They're very interested in his discovery. Some are actually terrified of it. You've acted as a buffer, allowing him to keep working while you both got rich off it. None of this is secret where I come from."

"Where is that exactly?" Anderson said.

Sorenson gestured at Durjaya and said, "Why don't you tell him?"

"What's he talking about, governor? Who's Ford Martin?" Anderson said.

Durjaya waved both men quiet, buying a moment to collect his thoughts. A piece of melting ice clinked in his scotch. He took a drink.

"Well, looks like I owe you an apology, Andy. This work with Martin has been beyond top secret, which is why you've been kept out of the loop." Durjaya tapped his camera implant. "It's all recorded but then redacted by order of the last three presidents. What Mr. Sorenson is getting at is that he's traveled here from the future."

"You're kidding," Anderson said.

"No, Andy. Martin's research is all about time travel," Durjaya said. "It's not the kind you're thinking of—no flashing lights and shiny machines. No leapfrogging willy-nilly through history. Martin's processes work at a neural level."

"Martin's a genius," Sorenson said. "His work becomes vital in the future. It's our lifeline, our one channel to the most pivotal figure in human history, our only chance to prevent a catastrophe. Governor Durjaya, please, listen to me. Make the right choice. Save nine billion lives."

"I need another drink." Anderson passed Sorenson to the bar, where he refilled his tumbler and took a long swallow. "Explain how this all works because I think you can both understand why I might be a tad skeptical."

"I know it's hard to accept, Andy," Durjaya said. "You should've seen my reaction the first time Ford spun it all out for me. But I've seen it firsthand and experienced it to some degree. Martin's ideas grew from a theory of his about how experience becomes memory, how our brain learns, how our cells and neural pathways form and change over time. I don't understand the science, but the basic concept is that time travel is possible at a quantum level by backing the mind up to points in the past, at which the traveler can either be equipped with the knowledge he didn't originally have at the time or influenced to act differently than he did the first time around. You can relive moments of your life and change them. You can be *made* to change them. Sounds like the ultimate head-trip, but here's the catch: changing a person's experience of past events changes the events themselves and all their consequences. Martin calls it the Principle of Subjectivity. It has to do with how occurrences are only fully realized when experienced. Beyond that, it's all down to a notebook-length equation mapping the space-time/sensory interface, which unless you have an advanced physics degree makes about as much sense as Latin to a cat."

"You're saying Sorenson has really traveled here from the future?" Anderson said.

"Not physically, no," Durjaya said. "Martin says that's impossible."

"You have no idea what we've built on Martin's foundation," Sorenson said. "Do you think the Wright Brothers envisioned the Space Shuttle, that Babbage foresaw the Internet? Technology progresses. We've gone much further than Martin did."

"Ford told me once," Durjaya said, "that moving backward in time/experience worked because the neural structures already exist or had existed. It's not possible to go forward because those pathways don't yet exist and might never be formed."

"So, Sorenson is trapped in our time?" Anderson asked.

"Not at all," Sorenson said.

"It's only his mind that's returned," Durjaya said, "with knowledge from the future and instructions reprogramming him in this era. So, tell me, Mr. Sorenson, what exactly am I going to do to turn the people against me?"

"I won't say because a chance exists that if you agree to drop out of the race right now, you'll act differently. But it's a lurid, violent episode that'll remain unknown to the public if we don't expose it," Sorenson said, "and Ford Martin's research along with it. We're prepared to do both, the moment it happens."

"How can anything like that happen in secret?" Anderson said. "The governor is in full compliance with Reston-McGarvey. His honesty rig is on at all times."

"They redacted Ford Martin. You think he won't redact whatever he wants once he's president? You think politicos like him don't find every possible way to game the system? The media won't even question what he says because they believe in the safeguards, just like you. No one wants to contemplate that those protections are corrupted."

Anderson snorted. "You don't know Governor Durjaya. He's a good man, the best of us."

"You're naïve," Sorenson said.

Moving with surprising speed, the governor threw his glass into Sorenson's face. Anderson took the cue and lunged forward from behind the bar. He grabbed the man's gun arm, shoving it toward the ground, and thrust his right shoulder into Sorenson's nose, cracking it. The gun fired twice with an odd, muffled report as Anderson tried to wrestle it free, then Governor Durjaya smashed the computer monitor, corner first, against Sorenson's head. Sorenson yelped then crumpled to his knees, and Durjaya kicked him in the jaw with all his might, snapping him onto his back. Anderson staggered then fell atop him, dead weight.

Durjaya rolled his chief of staff onto his back and dragged him clear of Sorenson. Blood spilled from two wounds in Andy's chest, a steady stream of crimson soaking his white shirt. In one hand, he clutched Sorenson's weapon.

"Hang on, Andy," the governor said. "Hang on, son."

"Stop... Sorenson..." Andy sputtered.

Sorenson, stunned and groggy, took advantage of their distraction to crawl toward the far corner of the room. The governor grabbed the gun from Anderson and turned it on its owner.

"Who sent you?" Durjaya said.

Sorenson scrambled on all fours until he struck the wall. He reached inside his jacket, pulled out a shining box of chrome and glass, and activated it. The device emitted a faint, bronze shimmer that produced a vertiginous effect. Durjaya staggered under its influence, then he fired, the gun barking once. When the slug hit Sorenson's chest, the box fell from his hand, and the light faded. Blood spouted from Sorenson's wound, and he slumped over. Governor Durjaya bent to one knee and inspected the box. He slid it into the pocket of his suit jacket.

"Governor...?" Anderson said.

"All right, Andy, take a deep breath. It's over," Durjaya said.

"What...?"

"This is your first encounter with the newest branch of politics," Durjaya said. "Sonofabitch, but I thought I had a lock on it. That fucker Martin better not be double-dealing me."

"Sorenson... *is* from the future?" Anderson gasped, coughed, and clutched at his wounded chest.

"Sort of, but not from a century out. No. He thought he was, maybe, but more likely, someone about six or seven years ahead of us rewired him to think so and set him up with that gun and the knowledge to make that box, which controlled which consciousness ruled his mind, and sent him to us. Our opposition, no doubt, using Martin's technology to take me off the board early. Dammit, maybe a mole in Martin's lab got them the tech needed to rig this guy. Sorenson couldn't have been from the time period he claimed. If that were true, he wouldn't have been alive in this era. No body, no neural pathways to absorb the new knowledge or altered experience. After this, there'll be no Sorenson even six or seven years from now, so on one level, he succeeded in changing the future."

"You... sure?"

"The probability of someone surpassing Martin's work is infinitesimal. There's a bit of risk involved in my assumption, but the odds are overwhelmingly in my favor. This attempt was clumsy. The next one won't be. Sorenson should've shot me to take me off the board. Maybe someone wanted him to do that, but influencing past personas is an art, not a science. If he wasn't a killer, to begin with, it'd be an uphill battle to make him one. Or maybe they didn't want to make me a martyr."

"What if... you're wrong? What if you do... cause all that death?" Anderson said, wondering why the governor seemed so calm, so still.

Durjaya flashed a surprised look at his chief of staff. "Andy, you and I are in the business of setting the world's course. Every decision we make involves the risk we're heading down a path that'll end somewhere we don't like. Goes with the territory. As long as the people stand behind us, our best efforts ought to be enough. Who cares what happens thirty years after I die? Why would I trade two terms in power as a beloved leader to protect the lives of people who can never vote for me?"

"Call... ambulance. I... need... help..." Anderson said.

"I know, Andy."

Anderson read the truth in Durjaya's sad, ambivalent eyes. "Eight years ago...?"

Durjaya nodded. "I hoped you'd never cotton on, but you've got a wonderfully sharp mind. Remember what I said about winning over one man completely? You don't think all my supporters came to me on their own, do you? Or that I got my reputation for winning over my opponents' supporters by charm alone? My platform from before Reconstitution made any comeback impossible unless I took drastic measures. It's amazing how easy it is to have all the right positions on all the right issues when you can influence enough people to think the way you want them to. We started with Robinson and the Illinois group. You can't imagine how quickly people agreed to change their stance when offered a chance to alter their past, or even just their perception of it."

"No. We made... you..." Anderson said, his voice feeble now.

"No, Andy, *I* made me," Durjaya said. "I made me, and I made *you*, too, and a hell of a lot of those mindless drones out there in the arena. We want the people to stand behind us, but sometimes we have to tell them where to stand."

"Governor... please... call help..." Anderson's voice dropped, low and breathy.

"I'll miss you, Andy. You're a loyal bastard, and we came a long way together. Don't think I don't appreciate it. If it's any consolation, by tomorrow morning, Martin will be planting seeds five years ago to make sure your death is mourned as a national tragedy. It'll be worth a lot of votes. I wouldn't want to become one myself, but a martyr is a powerful thing. I'll ride your assassination for years, and for that—and everything else you've done for me—I'm profoundly grateful."

"Your... honesty rig," Anderson said.

"Redacted." Durjaya tapped his left temple. "First order of business when I began my work with Ford: control the minds of the honesty monitors."

Bitterness flooded Anderson's darkening mind, but another sense chased them away; a peacefulness swept his hot emotions away and replaced them with the cool contentment of a job well done. The feeling disgusted him.

"Fuck you..." Anderson said, "how deep... did you go... in my head?"

Governor Sam Durjaya met Anderson's watery eyes and shrugged. He threw the gun into Sorenson's lap and pulled the shining box from his pocket. "I think Ford will be interested to see this little doohickey," he said. "Don't you, Andy?"

He tucked it back in his jacket, opened the door, and hollered for help. Korgi Anderson looked into the faces of three confused and horrified security guards pushing into the room. Governor Durjaya snapped orders, his voice fading into the rush of blood in his head, and then Anderson's past, present, and future crashed together, entwined in a terrible, black, constricting knot, as he became a campaign casualty.

Against the Stars Themselves

"...he had risen up out of the blackness of twenty-seven centuries, and... he had heard messages from places not on this planet."

—"Nyarlathotep," H.P. Lovecraft (1920)

The silver ship shuddered. Its nuclear engines burned to life, correcting its course against the pull of the nearby Moon's gravity.

Within the cold metal skin, Coleman Chang awoke and swatted at the flutterby hovering and beeping by his temple. He raised himself on his elbows and blinked the deep, cold dryness from his eyes. Beyond the nearest viewport, icy stars sped by amidst the black void.

None of the others had survived. The monitor lights at the base of their suspension tubes all flashed blue. Coleman knew the entire crew, himself included, had been expected to perish, but he'd harbored secret hopes of beating the odds. Not that any of them mattered. Only the data mattered, and that rested securely in the belly of the craft.

Coleman pushed back the glass seal and shifted out of his tube. His flutterby withdrew, the blue disc floating a standard three feet behind his left shoulder, its devices scanning his vital signs, recording his every move. The blue discs of the others lay cold upon the steel and glass cocoons that had become their coffins.

Fifteen years, Coleman thought. *I'm going home alone.*

Out of those fifteen years, he'd spent perhaps one fully conscious, with six months alone dedicated to the team's research, completing work only possible during the period when their seemingly infinite, preprogrammed trajectory carried them within range of Pluto and the mysterious celestial body beyond. Near enough to run scans and measurements from within their vessel. Did the knowledge gained justify the deaths of six men and women, Coleman's friends and colleagues? He didn't know. He served only as messenger, the value of the data well beyond his judgment.

The hum of the engines faded, and the ship plummeted onward in heavy silence toward Earth. Coleman entered the tiny cockpit and commenced the required diagnostic routines. All systems checked out. With luck, the *Marathon* would approach Earth orbit in less than two days. Until then, he would wait in the cramped and cold cockpit. He preferred that to returning to the sleep chamber. He wished for a book or music to soothe his restlessness, anything to distract his mind from the enormity of their undertaking and the sheer horror that demanded their sacrifice.

Coleman tried to pin the start down to a single event, but there were too many. What had happened seemed the inevitable confluence of history—and he had no idea how history might have changed during his long absence.

In his lifetime alone, humanity had weathered riots led by men and women who'd succumbed to madness and degenerated to a primitive state of bloodlust, thousands of cultists burning the cities, murdering all those they could. Humanity trembled in the grip of raw violence for nine dark days before order returned as thirty, fifty, a hundred nations enacted martial law to stamp out the erupting savagery. Coleman turned seven years old that year.

Five years later, twelve-year-old Coleman followed the news, transfixed, as the Black Armies of Kavage Kash rolled forth from the deserts of Africa and marched in conquest across Persia into Asia and Europe. They bore strange weapons: massive, glowing contraptions and dirty, soot-coated machines hauled on heavy trailers to spread poisons and disease. They held great cities hostage, bent once-powerful nations to their will, and it seemed soon the entire world would fall beneath their ruthless on-slaught. Then came a fleet of planes bearing immense bombs and the most crucial armament, information. A shard of luck had revealed the location of the Black Armies' leader, and so his enemies cut loose the head of the beast, obliterating him and all life surrounding him for twenty miles.

Some claimed Kavage Kash served only as a figurehead for the true power behind the Black Armies. Small circles of cynical men whispered of a dark and powerful leader, who traveled in mystery surrounded by a fog of panic. In his mind, they said, dwelled the secrets of ultimate chaos and despair and that his hidden connivances edged the world ever closer toward an unyielding abyss. Where he walked, cities screamed in the night.

From the dust of the Black Armies' destruction, abhorrent, deformed creatures spilled forth from the sea, rising to attack lonely ships on open waters. Rumors circulated of isolated communities of men who were no longer men but hideous beasts who'd forfeited their humanity for terrible profits. Perversions lurked behind the doors of even the most respectable families, and the rulers of the world were revealed as utterly bankrupt of conscience.

At age eighteen, Coleman joined the military. Five years later, he volunteered to lead six others on a fearful journey further into the depths of the cosmos than any other person had ever traveled.

In his last earthbound days, his grandfather bid him farewell. The old man spoke of times past when smoke and blackness did not fill the skies, when men still cherished the idea of living in peace because they fought only among each other. He recalled arriving in his adopted country, his soul swelling with pride and determination to build a new life. Many of Grandfather Chang's generation surrendered their sanity in the face of the changed world. "Bleak" and "hopeless," they called it, an "abomination of life," but to Coleman, who'd never known it otherwise, it was only the world. He marveled at the confidence in his progenitor's voice, speaking of subjects that caused others to tremble with emotion.

"You're doing a noble thing, Coleman. It's a fitting way to define yourself," said the elder Chang. "But the universe has its plan for us, and the power of men—whatever role we are meant to play—may be insufficient to alter it. Fate will make us its agents, willing or not."

Coleman wished his grandfather could've lived long enough to greet him when he returned.

The *Marathon* had lifted off before dawn on a hot summer morning. The resources of the entire nation supported the vessel's construction. The seven-person crew underwent two months of the most intense training Coleman ever experienced. Although they'd spend most of the trip unconscious, they could leave no margin for error during their active period. Each crew member fulfilled a vital function, and they would get no second chances. Given more time, the scientists might have perfected the suspension tubes in which the crew would sleep, but time was an empty well. The crew left, knowing no test subject had ever survived a second stint in suspension. One way only, no return.

Coleman thought of the feverish passion that had burned in President Aldrich's eyes, the glow of physical energy and iron will that had surrounded that barrel-chested man when he spoke, as though secrets within him burst to break free. Three nights before departure, he brought Coleman and the crew by helicopter from their training base in Virginia to an isolated valley in the mountains of Pennsylvania. There, Aldrich transported them deep beneath the surface through the labyrinthine tunnels of an abandoned mine until they entered an underground complex, where he gathered them into an observation room overlooking a darkened chamber.

Lights flared to life. Coleman and the others flinched in disgust from the vast, fetid mass that churned below them. It moved like a single-minded beast, but its body writhed like a bundle of thick worms fused together at the tails. A strand of the thing smacked upward and caressed the heavy window, smearing a sticky trail of smoking slime on the glass. The sight sent cold dread flowing through Coleman. He had faced horrors in the line of duty, mutations and feral killers, demonic creatures and foul, pathetic cannibals, but none so fundamentally repulsive as this.

Aldrich couldn't identify the thing or say where it had come from, or even if it possessed intelligence. A recovery team had seized it from a Navy destroyer found adrift in the Indian Ocean. Fifty-three men died to transport it in an empty oil tanker and bring it inland. Aldrich revealed it to Coleman and the others to prepare them. "It's only right," he said, "that you who are about to give your lives should know firsthand what we're fighting. Life exists out where you're going and in other dimensions where man should never venture. There are, well, dormant entities present on Earth, even now, and they see humanity the same way we see vermin. Or maybe insects. Or microbes, for all we know. They're stirring. We think they mean to reclaim our world where they once ruled as masters."

Aldrich led them through the complex to other rooms where scientists studied alien metals in laboratories that stank like graves, where learned men ruminated over the enigma of ancient works penned on paper and skins now desiccated and fragile, where generals plotted their resistance. These men pried at the locks on the occult knowledge that would guide them as they schemed for the freedom of mankind on Earth. Coleman's team would take the first steps toward securing freedom for humanity in the universe. Their investigation would determine the truth of disparate ancient writings that heralded a benighted body beyond the ninth planet as home to otherworldly beings. And so they had done.

Coleman assembled a mental picture of the icy, inexplicable mass they had encountered, the horrifying structures that dotted its surface, the slowly spinning black forms that covered miles of ground, and the tiny, wriggling figures that flitted through the air. Sickly-colored gasses filled its atmosphere, shot through by bolts of carmine lightning. Jets of emerald flame flared from great crevasses in the planetary crust. A ring of shining, black bodies, like demonic idols carved from obsidian, orbited the equator, the sleeping guardians of a veiled world. Most of the crew viewed the high-resolution camera images of the surface. Coleman learned all he cared to know about the visions of Hell they'd dredged up from the expressions on the faces of people he knew as fearless. He cared only about completing the mission.

A flutterby chirped, stirring him from his nightmarish ruminations.

In the blackness ahead loomed a shining craft Coleman identified as a starship, though he'd never seen its like before. It blotted out the heavens. Coleman's fingertips hammered at the course controls, but his ship remained locked on its heading.

The radio crackled with a familiar voice. "This is President Aldrich to the *Marathon*. Do you read me?"

The words, the *voice*, stunned Coleman. His heart brimmed with feeling. Aldrich repeated his greeting twice more before Coleman mustered an answer.

"This is *Marathon*. Captain Coleman Chang here," he said.

"Coleman!" the president said. "My God, you're alive! Incredible. It's good to hear your voice, captain. What's your status?"

"Ship status, fine. All systems intact," Coleman said. "Crew status is... six members code blue."

"I'm sorry, son," Aldrich said. "But welcome home. We've taken over your craft by remote now. We'll guide her in. You relax. We'll have you up here in no time. You've done more than we could ever have hoped for, soldier."

What could have happened in fifteen years to place this ship here to meet him halfway between the Earth and the Moon? The *Marathon* embodied the peak of human technology when he left. How could his people have constructed such a vast machine in so short a time? Why did President Aldrich still hold office after so many years?

A dark portal blistered open on the hull of the massive starship. Coleman's craft floated into it, into dim lights and the glint of steel. The power of the immense thing thrummed all around him, then his ship emerged into the sterile glare of a hangar. He shaded his still-sensitive eyes and braced himself as the *Marathon* lowered to a soft touchdown. Coleman struggled for his bearings. Metal clanged as a tube connected to the craft's dorsal hatch. Minutes later, it creaked open. Two men appeared, garbed in tight-fitting environment suits. They helped Coleman from the cockpit.

He spent three hours in a small medical facility. Doctors dissected his flutterby and processed the data within. They conducted countless tests, took a dozen readings, drew blood and other fluids, flashed lights in his eyes, and poked, probed, and injected him. Finally, the physician cracked the seal on his mask, removed his headpiece, and with a smile, pronounced Coleman healthy.

"We're not sure why you survived your second suspension, captain, but you're no worse for the wear," the doctor said.

"Guess you got lucky. That old tech is unpredictable. Occasionally, it outperformed expectations. Of course, we've got all those bugs worked out these days. Freeze you and defrost you a hundred times, and you'd never feel a thing."

The doctor left, and Coleman sat alone for a while in the cold med chamber and thought of his lost companions. For him, only a day had passed since they had said goodbye.

Before long, a trio of soldiers escorted him through cramped corridors to a compact and austere room, where he sat on a plastic bench affixed to the floor. A garish piece of abstract art hung framed on the opposite wall. Coleman's eyes strained to make sense of the image. Then he realized it wasn't art at all but a map of the world. Here and there, he distinguished the shape of a familiar coastline or the outline of an inland body of water. But much had changed. He pictured the old world laid over this new configuration, and his head ached. He looked away, grateful for the distraction when a door swept back, and President Aldrich entered.

"I have no words to express how good it is to see you again, captain," Aldrich said. He took Coleman in a rough embrace and patted his back. "Many people want to speak to you, but I ordered them off. I want you to myself for now."

Aldrich had grown gaunt and frail. His hair had thinned and fallen out. A jagged scar disfigured his left cheek. His wide blue eyes, once crackling with life, were now stark and rheumy, and his hands trembled.

"I'm terribly sorry about your crew. If we'd had then the technology we have now... well, we're already analyzing the data your team retrieved. Excellent work, captain. Exactly one-hundred percent what we sent you out there to do. Of course, it's nothing we don't already know now. We've learned a great deal since you've been gone. But it's confirming the less definitive things Doctor Abgrund has theorized, and precise intelligence is key to a successful campaign."

"Mr. President, what campaign? Who's Doctor Abgrund?" Coleman asked.

Aldrich nodded. "Yes, I'm sorry, I'm getting ahead of myself. Don't wish to jar you. It's one of the reasons I made radio contact myself. Familiar voice. But we know so much more about the Old Ones now than we did when you left."

"The Old Ones?" Coleman asked, but Aldrich didn't seem to hear him.

"There aren't many people left on Earth, now—maybe a million per continent, counting those trapped in the Antarctic deserts. We kept a lid on things as long as possible. I mean, what kind of cover story can you devise when a sinkhole swallows Berlin and spews forth a host of demons? Civilization broke down. More of the things appeared. You remember the one I showed you? Some like that. Many much worse. North America hung on the longest, but then the sunken city rose, and no one could question the prophecies any longer. That's when Doctor Abgrund finally reached us and explained the massive tactical blunder we'd made so many years ago. We thought Kavage Kash and his Black Armies were the Crawling Chaos described by the ancient texts, the avatar destined to herald the apocalypse. But the Black Armies never meant to conquer the world. Abgrund had given them the weapons and technology to save it. We only weakened ourselves when we destroyed them. How many lives lost for our ignorance? Abgrund knows the Old Ones better than any of us. Once he served their cult during his youth in Egypt and Sudan, but when he realized the extent of their evil, he turned on them. His unique knowledge has been vital to implementing my contingency plans."

Aldrich rose and stood enrapt before the map of the world.

"I see the questions in your eyes, captain, the worry and the fear, the uncertainty. I can imagine how disorienting it is to jump fifteen years into the future.

"When I was a child, my father told me a story on his deathbed. He'd exhausted his life in the pursuit of perverse pleasures and forbidden delicacies, wasting his body as he spent his soul. How many awful secrets he took to the grave, I couldn't say, nor do I care to know. But with his final breaths, he whispered in my ear a message of terror—not of his own death—but of the doom awaiting all men. With those words, he redeemed himself. Through me, he saved humanity. He confided in me the location of a cache of books and materials he'd hidden and made me swear to take measures to protect myself against what I'd find expressed within them. The books were... difficult to understand... but I made out enough to realize I was meant to serve a greater purpose. I would save us all from the Old Ones who'd destroy our way of life and enslave us. My sole purpose became preparing for the coming battle. I acted in secret at first. Who'd believe such things until they were before their very eyes? I needed power enough to destroy them, and so I dedicated my life to obtaining it. Yes, I underestimated them in the past, but now I have all the force I need at my disposal."

"Sir?" Coleman said.

"I'd planned the ships since the first day I took office. This one. A hundred others like it. The technology didn't exist, but only the concept that mattered then. Abgrund provided the missing pieces of the technical puzzle. He perfected our suspension tubes and designed our engines. It was deemed vital to our success that I remain president until the crisis passed. When the sunken city emerged, we gathered all those we could onto the ships and ordered the strike. It lasted three days. We fired fifteen hundred missiles. We wiped their worshippers—those dirty, subhuman traitors—off the face of the Earth. We buried the pits from which they rose. We scattered their numbers and slew their minions. It wasn't enough. In the end, the sleeping city stood undamaged. It sank, again, beneath the waves after unleashing a psychic blast that left a billion mindless shells wandering our destroyed cities."

Aldrich rubbed his eyes as though very tired and chilled to the bone.

"Then I understood what we needed to do," he whispered.

"What, sir?" Coleman's voice quivered. The meaningless deaths of his friends paled before the anguish he felt hearing of his world brought to the brink of extinction, thinking of the grotesquely warped map, wondering who and what remained.

"You see, captain, the stars were in the wrong configuration. Doctor Abgrund erred in his calculations. He believed the time was right for such a massive strike, that we should have been able to destroy the city when it surfaced and thus eliminate the heart of the Old Ones' foothold on Earth. It appeared for only a short time, not long enough for its prisoner to fully rouse itself. Its protections remained intact. But when it sank again, it gave us the respite we needed. We don't know how long we have, but we have our plan settled. Abgrund has translated the ancient texts fully now, and we know that the stars must be in the proper alignment for the Old Ones to return. We know which stars are required."

Aldrich took Coleman's arm and helped him up from his seat.

"Within this vessel are hundreds of thousands of men and women locked in suspension tubes, and in fifty other ships, the same. Our journey will be long. Many will die. So, we have reinforcements, endless and waiting to be called upon, prepared to assert the will of mankind against the stars themselves. They are our future."

A cold light gleamed through the president's face. The idea of his race entombed in living death numbed Coleman. Aldrich gripped the captain's arm tighter and led him into an adjoining auditorium. Coleman experienced apprehension a thousand times worse than when Aldrich had long ago shown him the terrible beast. A wall-length portal afforded a view of Earth, but not the planet Coleman remembered. Thick black smoke and pulsing orange flame replaced its majestic blues and greens, and the ashy clouds roiled in tumultuous, lightning-seared swirls.

"We devastated the Earth to save it, Coleman," Aldrich said. "I won't let those countless deaths go unanswered. We must make sure mankind never falls prey to the Old Ones. This ship and its companions are capable of traveling beyond our solar system. Doctor Abgrund has led us light years beyond where we were when we built your little spacecraft."

Coleman followed the president down an aisle between the rows of plastic seats that filled the room, each one occupied by a man or woman, their bodies as worn and deteriorated as their leader's, a touch of madness in all of their eyes. They gazed at Coleman's clear expression, unblemished skin, and powerful body with a dangerous hunger.

On the dais before the viewport stood a tall man in a black uniform with hands the color of ash. A smooth, featureless, silver mask hid his face. Through its slits, his eyes flickered like sulfurous coals. They burned through Coleman. The effect dizzied him as though an invisible force reached out from the man to send Coleman's thoughts aflutter like a child running through a flock of feeding pigeons. Coleman averted his eyes, but his legs wavered.

"Captain Chang, please meet Doctor Abgrund," Aldrich said. "Together, he and I have become the architects of our survival and the champions of our freedom. Behold our works."

The starship rolled, and the fleet drifted into view—ten, thirty, fifty, and more ships like the one on which Coleman stood, hanging in the endless night. Mounted along their flanks hung innumerable steel spears like the weapons of a giant-killer, an arsenal of missiles with the power to turn space itself to embers. The ships dipped and swayed, a school of mechanical fish, orienting themselves for a long migration. Between them, as they shifted, Coleman glimpsed the ruined shell of the world he'd once called home.

"We'll make sure the stars can never be right," Aldrich said. "We'll destroy them."

The auditorium exploded with applause. Coleman's mind drained to emptiness in an instant. Through the darkness came only the simmering laughter of the man in the silver mask, a dissonant, vaguely musical whistling like the pressure of eternity forced through a narrow pipe that filled the void within him—and then he heard his own voice join in cheering on Aldrich's mission.

PREVIOUSLY PUBLISHED

"Against the Stars Themselves" first appeared in *The Black Book*, Peter Worthy, ed., January 2003.

"A Beach on Nellus" first appeared in *In Harm's Way*, (Defending the Future, Volume 8), Mike McPhail, ed., Pennsville, NJ: eSpec Books, 2019.

"The Black Box" first appeared in *Footprints in the Stars*, Mike McPhail, ed., Pennsville, NJ: eSpec Books, 2019.

"Father of War" first appeared in *Dogs of War* (Defending the Future, Volume 6), Mike McPhail, ed. Howell, NJ: Dark Quest Books, 2013.

"Killer Eye" first appeared in *Breach the Hull* (Defending the Future, Volume 1), Mike McPhail, ed., Marietta, GA: Marietta Publishing, 2007.

"Law of the Kuzzi" first appeared in *No Longer Dreams*, Danielle Ackley-McPhail, Lee Hillmann, L. Jagi Lamplighter, and Jeff Lyman, eds. Baltimore, MD: Lite Circle Books, 2005.

"War Movies" first appeared in *So It Begins*. (Defending the Future, Volume 2), Mike McPhail, ed., Howell, NJ: Dark Quest Books, 2009.

Byanntia, the Kuzzi, and related concepts and settings © Bruce Gehweiller.

About the Author

James Chambers is an award-winning author of horror, crime, fantasy, science fiction, and other genres. He wrote the Bram Stoker Award®-winning graphic novel, *Kolchak the Night Stalker: The Forgotten Lore of Edgar Allan Poe* and was nominated for a Bram Stoker Award for his story, "A Song Left Behind in the Aztakea Hills." *Publisher's Weekly* gave his Lovecraftian novella collection, *The Engines of Sacrifice*, a starred review and described it as "...chillingly evocative." He is the author of the short story collections *On the Night Border*, called "...a haunting exploration of the space where the real world and nightmares collide" by *Booklist*, and the collection *On the Hierophant Road*, of which *Booklist* said "fans of richly drawn, addictively compelling, speculative tales overflowing with dread and discomfort are in for a treat," in a starred review.

He has also written the collection *Resurrection House*, the Corpse Fauna novellas, and the dark urban fantasy novella, *Three Chords of Chaos*. His short stories have appeared in numerous anthologies, including *After Punk: Steampowered Tales of the Afterlife*, *The Averoigne Legacy*, *The Best of Bad-Ass Faeries*, *The Best of Defending the Future*, *Chiral Mad 2* and *4*, *Fantastic Futures 13*, *Footprints in the Stars*, *Gaslight and Grimm*, *The Green Hornet Chronicles*, *Hardboiled Cthulhu*, *Heroes of the Realm*, *In An Iron Cage*, *In Harm's Way*, *Kolchak the Night Stalker: Passages of the Macabre*, *The Pulp Horror Book of Phobias*, *Qualia Nous*, *Shadows Over Main Street (1 and 2)*, *The Spider: Extreme Prejudice*, *To Hell in a Fast Car*, *Truth or Dare*, *Walrus Tales*, *Weird Trails* and the magazines *Bare Bone*, *Cthulhu Sex*, and *Allen K's Inhuman*.

He co-edited the anthology, *A New York State of Fright: Horror Stories from the Empire State*, which received a Bram Stoker Award nomination and edited *Under Twin Suns: Alternate Histories of the Yellow Sign*. He has also written and edited comic books, including *Leonard Nimoy's Primortals*, "The Revenant" in *Shadow House*, and *The Midnight Hour* with Jason Whitley.

Visit his website: www.jameschambersonline.com.

All the Stars in Our Sky

Accelerator Ray
Alf Shupe
Andrew J Clark IV
Andrew Timson
Anita Morris
Anonymous
Anton Kukal
Bill Kohn
Bjorn Hasseler
Brad Jurn
Brendan Lonehawk
Brian Walker
Brooks Moses
Budding Dan
Carol Gyzander
Chand Svare Ghei
Christopher J. Burke
Craig "Stevo" Stephenson
Curtis and Maryrita Steinhour
Dale A Russell
Danielle Ackley-McPhail
Dave Hermann
David Lee Summers
David Sherman
David Stolarz
Ed Ellis
Elmi
Ergo Ojasoo
Evan L
Gary Phillips

Howard J. Bampton
Hrvoje Bukša
Ian Harvey
IdleDice
Isaac 'Will It Work' Dansicker
Ixias
Jacen Leonard
Jack Campbell
Jakub Narębski
Jason Rhine
Jennifer L. Pierce
Jeremy Audet
Jim Gotaas
JoanneBB
Joe M.
Joel Jefferson
John Fallon
John Idlor
John L. French
John T. Sapienza, Jr.
Jonathan Mendonca
Josh McGinnis
Joshua C. Chadd
Keith Hall
Keith Tracton
Keith West, Future Potentate
    of the Solar System
Kelly Pierce
Ken "Merlyn" Mencher
Ken Warner

Kerry aka Trouble
KJSP
L.E. Custodio
LetoTheTooth
Linda Pierce
maileguy
Marc "mad" W.
Mari Hersh-Tudor
Mark Newman
Marvin Langenberg
Matt & Ellie A
Mike Maurer
Mike Skolnik
Morgan Campbell
Morgan Hazelwood
ND Gray
Norman Jaffe
Otter Libris
P Anne Stevenson
Pepita Hogg-Sonnenberg
Peter D Engebos
pjk
Pook

Raphael Yedwab
Rob Steinberger
Robert C Flipse
Robert Claney
Sam Lubell
Sam Tomaino
Scott Schaper
Sergey Kochergan
Shervyn
Sheryl R. Hayes
Steph Parker
Stephen Ballentine
Steve Perry
Svend Andersen
Tasha Turner
Thomas Karwacki
Tina M Noe Good
Ty Drago
Vee Luvian
Will McDermott
Yakira Heistand